COOL CAT

Also by Jazz Taylor

Meow or Never

Starting from Scratch

COOL CAT

Jazz Taylor

SCHOLASTIC INC.

Copyright © 2024 by Jazz Taylor

All rights reserved. Published by Scholastic Inc., *Publishers since 1920*. SCHOLASTIC and associated logos are trademarks and/or registered trademarks of Scholastic Inc.

The publisher does not have any control over and does not assume any responsibility for author or third-party websites or their content.

No part of this publication may be reproduced, stored in a retrieval system, or transmitted in any form or by any means, electronic, mechanical, photocopying, recording, or otherwise, without written permission of the publisher. For information regarding permission, write to Scholastic Inc., Attention: Permissions Department, 557 Broadway, New York, NY 10012.

This book is a work of fiction. Names, characters, places, and incidents are either the product of the author's imagination or are used fictitiously, and any resemblance to actual persons, living or dead, business establishments, events, or locales is entirely coincidental.

ISBN 978-1-339-02230-7

10 9 8 7 6 5 4 3 2 1   24 25 26 27 28

Printed in the U.S.A.   40
First printing 2024

Book design by Omou Barry

To Grandma, every time.

And to all the girls who wear masks
the world created—I hope you find the people
who love the you behind them.

CHAPTER 1

See, here's the thing: Math is evil and should be abolished in schools everywhere.

What do we even need math for? I mean, of course we need it for money and stuff. But do we really need to know the area of a circle? Is there ever a time when Bri and I'll be at the park, and a shark will come out of the lake to eat us, and the only way to save ourselves is to know the circumference of a sphere?

I hope Bri knows how to save us, 'cause I sure don't.

Despite the pointlessness of math, I pull my curly hair back into a messy bun and stretch, then attack the next problem anyway. Because I *want* to understand math. I want to be able to fight off math sharks, if they exist. And I really want Mom to be proud, and she won't be unless I get all As in everything.

I scribble in my math notebook for a whole hour, and honestly all I can say is my wrist hurts now. I don't get it. When there's a formula, I always pick the wrong one. And then if there's a multistep problem, I can never remember the right order. I groan and rub my face with my hands. I really wish I'd taken regular math instead of geometry.

My phone lights up at my desk. Bri's picture pops up on the screen, but there's no sound. I'm not supposed to have my phone out during homework time, but I really need a break . . . and if Mom doesn't know about it, it can't hurt, right?

I answer, and Bri's face appears. She's too close to the phone, so I'm looking at one big brown eye and the top of her forehead. She pulls back, grinning, and I see that she's in her room. And dressed in her private school uniform. I beat down the twinge of jealousy the gold and navy stripes bring and smile back instead.

"Novaaaaa! I have to tell you something right now."

"Okay, but I'm trying to—"

"I saw the *biggest* dog I've ever seen in my life today."

Oh, this is way more important than math. "What kind?!"

"I don't know! It was so white and fluffy! Hold on, I'm sending you a picture."

A few seconds later, the biggest, fluffiest dog I've ever seen pops up over Bri's face. It has a creamy white coat, a black nose, and it's almost as tall as Bri's chest! And she's pretty tall, taller than me at least. "I need to meet this dog right now."

"Right?" Bri gushes. "His name is Porridge. I asked Mami if we could get one to be friends with Carl, but she said he was way too big."

Carl is Bri's weenie dog. He's not nice and bites us all the time, so even though he's cute, Bri is always asking for another dog. But he doesn't bite her mom, so there's no luck so far.

"You should just get a cat instead." I look around for Kevin, my cat. I find him snoozing in my closet, passed out on a pile of dirty socks. He's always stealing and hiding them, so I never have a matching pair. It's okay, though. Kevin is worth missing a few socks.

I found Kevin a year ago. I'd been begging Mom for a kitten for forever, but when I saw Kevin, already an old-man cat, wet and cold on my neighbor's porch, I had to have him. It took me almost two months to coax him inside with cat food and tuna fish sandwiches, but after that he never wanted to leave. Mom pretends she doesn't like him, but I catch her feeding him that gross cat Go-Gurt all the time.

"No way," Bri says. "Kevin is the only cat for me."

Kevin's ears twitch when Bri says his name. He looks up, blinking slowly, then yawns. I call him and he stands and waddles toward me. He rubs his head against my knee, and I scratch his ears. Kevin is the only cat for me too.

"What're you doing?" Bri asks. "I got distracted by the dog."

"Math." I let out a heavy sigh and Kevin tries to jump into my lap. *Tries* because he's really fat now and can't get himself off the floor. Indoor living really suits him. I pick him up so he doesn't claw my leg, and I put him in my lap. He closes his eyes and purrs.

"Gross." Bri sits at her desk, and I'm momentarily staring at the ceiling while she picks up papers and note cards. "We're doing proportions right now. Are you still doing shapes and stuff?"

"Yeah. I hate it." What I really hate is that Bri and I can't complain about math together because she goes to a different school now. She goes to a private school, one where they have to wear fancy uniforms (with ties!), and you have to be super-smart to get in. I think I'm smart, or at least I thought I was. Bri and I took a test to get into Harvest Hills Academy together, but she got in and I didn't. It stings, especially at night when I'm having nightmares about disappointing Mom, but what's worse is that I don't have any friends at school now that Bri's gone. I try not to worry about it, though, because I have a plan to fix all that. And, unfortunately, it requires defeating some evil math sharks.

"That's okay," Bri says. "We can study next Saturday! And then afterward we can get ice cream."

That cheers me up. Bri and I meet every other weekend because she still lives close, even if she's not with me every day.

"Okay. And maybe we'll see Porridge—"

"Nova!" Mom bellows from downstairs. "Dinnertime!"

Kevin shoots from my lap like a rocket. He doesn't know many words, but he definitely knows *dinner*. I laugh. "I gotta go."

"Okay! See you Saturday!" Bri blows me a kiss before hanging up.

I end the video call and run downstairs. Mom is in the kitchen, mumbling curses at Kevin because he keeps winding around her legs to get to the food. "Nova! Come get this cat."

Uh-oh. Annoyance drips from her words and she looks tired. I don't ever want to bother her on days like this. I pick up Kevin and carry him out of the kitchen, ignoring his yowls of protest.

"Can't even have dinner," Mom grumbles. But she brightens a little when she puts two boxes of pizza on the table and two bottles of water. "I got your favorite."

My stomach sours at that. I place Kevin down in his time-out box. It's just a baby playpen with a lid on it, but if we don't put him in here, he'll steal our food. He loves bread more than anything in the world. I take a deep breath. "Pepperoni?"

"Yes, ma'am! Now wash your hands and come sit down."

That's what I was afraid of. I hold in a sigh and wash my hands at the kitchen sink, ignoring Kevin yelling like we're starving him, and sit at the table. Mom has already picked two slices of pepperoni for me and put them on a paper plate. I stifle a groan as I stare down at it.

Pepperoni *used* to be my favorite. But last year I read an enlightening book on the meat industry and greenhouse gases, and meat didn't make me hungry anymore. I decided to become a vegetarian, and I feel a lot better about my impact on the world, but . . . I haven't exactly told Mom yet. It's awkward! No one else at school is a vegetarian, no one I know, anyway. And sometimes I hear adults sneering about "hippies," and it doesn't sound nice when they say it. So I just decided not to say anything. It's not so bad. I can just pick my pepperoni off. And . . . have to eat the horrible meat juice they leave behind on my soggy cheese. I stare forlornly down at my pizza. This might be another night of going hungry.

"What's wrong?" Mom asks.

I look up to answer, but then I spy her plate—two pieces of perfect, plain cheese. I gape at her food. She normally always gets supreme, which is almost worse than straight pepperoni. "Why do you have cheese pizza?"

"No coupons this time." Mom sighs and rubs the bridge of her nose. She's definitely tired today. "Toppings are more expensive, and I wanted to get pepperoni for you."

My heart softens. Mom is always looking out for me. That's why I do everything to make her happy and make sure I don't disappoint her. But this time, there's a way for us both to be happy! "Let's swap."

Mom's eyes widen in surprise. "Why? You love pepperoni."

"I want you to have it. I'm in a cheese mood today." I push my plate forward before she has a chance to question it and snag her plate with my fingernail. I drag it to me, and she seems confused but shrugs.

"Okay, if you're sure." Mom takes a bite of my gross pepperoni pizza and I barely contain a victory dance. The night is saved! No sneaking snacks at three a.m. while Mom is asleep! I take a bite of my hard-won cheese pizza, and it tastes better than any pizza I've ever had.

"How was school?" Mom asks after a few minutes of eating. She has to raise her voice over Kevin's wailing.

I try not to fidget under her gaze. "It was okay." I don't like telling Mom about school. It's boring. And lonely without Bri. But Mom can't bring Bri back and I can't go to the private school, so there's no point in mentioning it. Plus, she's already tired, and I don't want to make her day any worse.

Mom watches me carefully. She's got the Laser Eyes, which make me nervous. I feel like she can see right through me, into my heart and brain and maybe even through my bones.

"And how is math going?"

"Great! I got an A on my quiz." Except, I didn't get an A. I got a B, and a pretty low one at that. Mom still has her Laser Eyes, but I've gotten pretty good at avoiding them. Like a spy in a movie, dodging the red alarm beams. You just have to make sure your face is completely relaxed and you sound confident, no matter what you're saying. Bri says I'm a pathological liar, but I don't like to think of it as lying. I'm just being hopeful about the future. If I keep working hard in math—which I *will*—eventually I will get an A on a quiz. So it's not lying, it's just like . . . future sight. Clairvoyance! We learned that as a vocab word in English last week. Mom would be proud that I remembered it.

Mom stares at me for a few more seconds, then puts the Laser Eyes away. Whew. I made it through, and now I can get the diamond, like spies do. But my diamond is just pizza.

"I'm glad to hear that." Mom nods to herself and nibbles thoughtfully on a piece of crust. She didn't use to eat the crust, but lately she has, and getting less pizza. "Grades are important, Nova. If you slack off now, you'll pay for it later."

I wince. I know. And I'm trying hard, I really am, but I just don't get math like I used to . . . no, that's just an excuse. I have to work harder, and then Mom'll be proud and she'll forgive me for not getting into private school like Bri. Everything will be fine.

I open my mouth to change the subject, but I hear an awful noise—the sound of the lid of Kevin's time-out box clattering to the ground. Before I can move, Kevin comes barreling right for me and my pizza.

Kevin leaps onto the table, scattering our plates and forks. I squeal and grab my plate, just seconds before he chomps on it.

"Mom! He escaped!"

But Mom is just kind of laughing. Normally she'd be so mad at Kevin, but she's smiling! I haven't seen her smile like that since we found out about Harvest Hills Academy. I'm so shocked, I freeze.

Kevin takes advantage of my distraction and sinks his front claws into the biggest piece of cheese pizza on my plate. I grab the other side, but he won't let go.

"Mom! Help!"

But Mom doesn't help. She has her phone out instead, pointed right at Kevin. I'm starting to get mad. He'll gobble up the best slice and she's not doing anything about it. I wrestle with Kevin, but I know I've lost when he bites into the crust. He jerks his head and makes off with a huge chunk of the crust and part of the cheese.

"Kevin! I'm gonna get revenge!" I yell at his retreating back as he gallops into the hall with his prize. I sit in my chair in a huff, defeated, and look at Mom. She still has her phone out, and it's pointed right at me. "Are you recording this?"

Mom chuckles and taps a button on her phone. "Not anymore."

I fold my arms. "You could have helped."

"I know." Mom smiles at me, a rare, gentle one. "You always look so happy when you play with that cat. I'm glad we kept him."

I smile back. Mom must be in a better mood after eating the pepperoni. She's always working and tired, so I do everything I can to make sure I don't bother her. Maybe this was worth one stolen slice of pizza.

We finish eating what's left after Kevin's attack and clean up the kitchen. I go to my room so Mom can do some of her after-work work (she's going to college online! She and Bri are the smartest people I know), and when I get upstairs, my phone has a notification.

Mom: *Thought you'd like to have this :)*

Attached is the video she took of me and Kevin. It's not long, just twenty seconds, but it is pretty funny. And the best part is I can hear Mom laughing in the background.

I smile at it for a while. Then, I stand up and close the door before settling on my bed. I go to my hidden apps that you can't see from the Home Screen and tap on Instagram.

I'm not supposed to have an account. I know I'm too young, and Mom really doesn't want me to have social media. But Bri has one, and I like to see what her new school looks like. And her new friends. And I hardly ever post pictures of myself; most of them are really bad pictures of Kevin because he hates the camera. So I don't think it's a bad thing to have an Instagram! Mom is just being too paranoid.

I post the video, with "Kevin the thief >:(" as the caption. I like some pictures from Bri's Instagram, plus some art people I follow. Then I put down my phone and sit at my desk. It's nine o'clock now, but I can't go to bed until I defeat some math sharks.

I put my hair up again and get back to work.

CHAPTER 2

I'm having a really good dream.

I know it's a dream because I'm in the same uniform Bri wears (the cute tie!), and there's no math anywhere to torture me. I'm in the park, sitting on a swing, and a big fluffy dog pushes me with his giant head. I go higher and higher, laughing, and a bunch of nameless, faceless friends surround the swings and cheer me on. Their cheers start encouraging but grow kind of annoying, a rhythmic screeching sound almost, but I ignore that and focus on beating the world record for highest leap from the swings—

"Nova!"

The screeching sound stops. I blink and I'm back in my room. Wait, I'm in my room?

"Nova, what are you doing?!" Mom yells. That wakes me up. I sit up in bed, panicked, while Mom glares down at me. She's holding my phone, which is traitorously silent. "It's seven fifteen! You'll miss the bus!"

The bus comes at seven thirty! I scramble out of bed, apologizing to Mom as I brush my teeth and pull on my school clothes at the same time. Kevin watches from the doorway, purring and sitting on my jeans. Thanks, Kevin, for keeping them warm. I tug them from under his bowling ball body and jam my legs in while trying to put deodorant on with my other hand. Ugh, why did I oversleep?! Mom hates it when I miss the bus because it makes her late for work and ruins her day. I stayed up really late studying, but I thought for sure I'd wake up with my alarm . . .

I must break the speed record for getting ready for school, but I run downstairs without my backpack and have to go back up to get it. By the time I fling open my front door, the bright yellow bus is already at the end of the street, headed to school without me.

I pant in my driveway, lungs heavy and full of icy winter air. I'd run outside before I knew it, like I could actually outrun the bus. Now I feel silly *and* sad. I turn to Mom, who's standing at the door, my eyes already full of tears. She rubs her face with one hand and sighs. "Get in the car."

The ride to school is torture. Mom is silent and I try to hide my frustrated tears so she won't see. I hate it when this happens. Now she'll be late for work, and she'll be stressed out because of me. Why'd I have to oversleep? Why do I always get everything wrong?

I wipe my eyes as Mom pulls into the drop off car line. I have to be normal, so Mom won't worry about me on top of everything else. I hop out when she stops, but I hesitate before closing the door.

"Mom? I'm really sorry. I'll wake up extra early tomorrow."

Mom finally looks at me. She still seems irritated, but it's a lot softer than earlier. Still pretty bad, because she shouldn't be mad at all and it's all my fault she is. "It's okay, Nova, but you have to be more responsible from now on. Have a good day."

I wince at the "responsible" part. I'm trying, but . . . no, I know trying to wake up isn't the same as actually waking up on time. It's just not good enough. I want her to say "I love you" like she would on a normal day, but I don't push it. I just nod and close the car door, and I feel lower than I have in a while.

I know I said math should be abolished, but today I'm thinking school should be too.

When I get to my first class, English, I feel worse. Piper says hi to Darrius, Lexi gushes about her crush to Bethany, Kylie looks cool while two other kids compliment her new pink-and-purple jumpsuit (which is pretty cool, not going to lie). But no one talks to me. No one approaches my desk. Because since Bri left, I've had a hole in school that no one can fill.

I don't like to say I have *zero* friends at school. I can ask Lexi for an eraser if I forget mine, or Piper for an extra pencil. But they're just school friends. Bri was my *real* friend. Real friends know you're a vegetarian and aren't doing great in math and come to your birthday party. I'm turning thirteen in three months, but I don't have anyone I'd invite to my birthday party except for Bri. Mom probably wouldn't allow me to invite anyone else anyway, but that's not the point. The point is I don't have any real friends at school I could even get anxious about asking, and that sucks.

I push away the sadness from this morning's fiasco and missing Bri as I go through the school day. It's better if I focus on school, which I'm good at. English wants me to read a sad dog book—easy. I've already read it and cried buckets. Science wants me to read about buoyancy—easy. That's just what makes things float in water, right? No problem. Home ec wants me to learn how to scramble eggs—I've scrambled eggs since I was seven! I'm feeling pretty confident all day until I get to geometry class. Then, all I feel is dread and fear.

Mr. Wickett is standing at the board when I walk in. He's a tall white man with a scruffy beard and dark brown eyes. He has Laser Eyes like Mom, but his are for searching for weak math points. If math sharks existed, he would have a hundred as pets.

"Good afternoon, Miss Harris," he says to me. His voice is very soft for such a big man. Maybe to lure students into a false sense of security before he gives us awful math problems.

"Hi, Mr. Wickett."

He nods in response and greets the people who come in after me. I sit at my desk and pull out my homework. I review it one more time, my stomach in knots. I hope it's all right. I worked so hard on it.

"Good afternoon, Miss Weston."

I look up and any leftover gloominess is blasted away. Lily Weston says hi to Mr. Wickett, and then she sits right next to me. She smiles at me and the knot in my stomach gets tighter, but this time in a good way.

I hate math, but there is one thing I like about it—and she's sitting right next to me.

Last year, in health class, we talked about puberty. Mrs. Helen explained that we might start getting pimples and grow hair in weird places and start our periods. And we might also start thinking that boys aren't so gross after all. The first three all happened to me—all according to plan, I guess. But I don't think boys are any less gross. I don't really think of them as anything special at all. But you know who I do think is special? Lily Weston. I like that her face is round and compliments her big brown eyes, and she's always confident in class, even in math. And she smells good and she's nice to everyone, even though she's super popular. And she wears mascara that makes her eyelashes look long and dark and beautiful. And when she smiles at me, my heart starts beating really fast and my palms get super sweaty. Which is not according to Mrs. Helen's plan.

Bri and I discussed this, and she thinks that I'm queer and I like girls. Maybe boys too, later, but not right now. I'm not sure about labels, but I know that when Lily looks at me, I feel like I might faint, in a good way. And that's enough for me right now.

"Hi, Nova," Lily says as she sits down.

"Hi" is all I manage to squeak out. I want to ask about the homework and how she did, if maybe we should study together sometime, and maybe we could go to the park sometime and get ice cream, but I can't do anything except smile weakly.

"This was really hard, huh?" She grimaces at her homework as she takes it out of her bright purple bag. "I don't get it at all."

This is my chance. I can do this. I take a shaky breath. "M-me neither."

Lily brightens when I finally speak. "I'm glad it's not just me! If the smartest kid in class is struggling, then I know it's just hard stuff."

Smartest kid? Me?! My face feels like someone set me on fire. Oh God, I hope she can't see me blush! I want to say something, but the bell rings and we all know better than to talk in Mr. Wickett's class. Mr. Wickett takes our homework from last night and gives back the homework from last week. Mine has a few red marks and a bright red 85 at the top. Ugh.

Something nudges my right leg, and it takes me five whole seconds to realize it's Lily's foot. I turn to look at her and she holds up her homework grade. A big red 75 on hers. She smiles and points at a tiny cluster of words at the bottom of her paper she wrote in pencil. It says: *Don't give up! It's just really hard.*

Even when Mr. Wickett starts chattering about how to use

the Pythagorean theorem, I can't help but grin at my paper all class long.

After school, I skip off the bus. Today started rough, and I got another B instead of an A in math, but Lily talked to me! And she wrote me a nice note! I'm about to float away.

I dig in my backpack for my key, and my stomach swoops in relief when I find it. Mom would be extra mad if she got home two hours later and I was still sitting on the porch. I used to stay with my neighbor, Mrs. Anderson, after school, but she moved to Florida last summer. Since then, Mom lets me stay by myself until she gets off from work. She was really anxious about it at first and forbade me from a lot of stuff, including having friends over while she's not home and touching the stove. But it's been fine—I don't need to touch the stove when the microwave is right there, and I don't have any friends anymore. It's very boring while I wait for her to get home.

Well, it was, until I started implementing my secret plan. I cuddle with Kevin until he gets tired, and then I open my door and step inside, making sure the door is locked behind me. It's a good thing Mom isn't here because I'd have a hard time explaining what I do in the two hours she's not home, which is work on getting into Bri's private school.

I've agonized about it for weeks, maybe even months, but I don't understand why I didn't get in. We had to do an interview thing, and mine went really well. Maybe it's because I don't have extracurriculars? Bri plays piano (though she hates it and wants to play saxophone instead) and volunteers through Girl Scouts. I don't have that, so all I can do is study. My idea is that if I get a perfect score on the entrance exam, they have to let me in, even if I can't play piano and only eat Girl Scout cookies rather than sell them. If I get into private school, everything will be solved. I'll have Bri as a friend again, and Mom will be proud of me and hopefully not be so stressed. So I have to get in. *I have to.*

The next entrance exam is in April, so I have two months left to study. And I've been getting ready. Every day from three to five I study advanced vocab words, how to write persuasive essays, and science. I've sort of been avoiding math, but honestly the last entrance exam had math that was doable. The science and vocab were the hardest parts, so I focus on that. It does eat into my regular homework time, but it's all worth it if I can be with Bri again. I just hope she still wants to be my friend when I get there.

That makes me think of Bri, and I resist the urge to scroll through her Instagram. She always posts about her new friends, Tiffany and Skylar, and what they're doing in their cool-looking science labs and eating their cool lunches. I'm not jealous, I swear, but what's so great about bento boxes anyway? Who cares if the rice is shaped like a bear when you're just gonna eat it?

Okay, I guess I am a *little* jealous. Bri and I don't talk about her new friends often, but I see them in her pictures all the time. Well, I see a lot of Skylar's elbows. He must be camera shy. We never take pictures together when we hang out, so on Instagram it looks like Bri's only friend is Tiffany. What about me? If I stop commenting and liking her posts, will she forget about me?

I glance at my phone uneasily. Maybe one look before exam prep won't hurt.

I flinch in surprise when Bri's picture pops up on my phone. I'm a little panicked—is she psychic?! And it's a phone call. Bri and I usually FaceTime. I answer the call, a little nervous.

"Hello?"

"Check your Instagram!" Bri yells in my ear. "Hurry, hurry!"

I put her on speaker and tap my Instagram. My mouth drops as I stare at it. And then I just stare at it some more. Because Kevin's video, the one of him stealing my pizza, has fifty thousand views.

"What . . . ?" I can't even speak. There are hundreds of comments and new followers. A hundred DMs. The comments are all laughing emojis and people telling me Kevin is cute.

I think my video has gone viral.

CHAPTER 3

I stare at my Instagram, mouth open like a fish. I keep looking at the numbers, but my brain can't make sense of them. Fifty thousand views. Hundreds of comments. A whole bunch of DMs. My phone won't stop buzzing with each new notification, and it feels like a giant bee vibrating in my palm. Slowly, a grin creeps onto my face. People like Kevin! They think he's funny! They're commenting cute things and sending pictures of their own orange cats. I won't have to lose to Bri in a pet picture competition ever again! I'm so popular now, I bet everyone will see the video—

Everyone, including Mom.

All my happiness dries up like a raisin in an Alabama summer.

"You're famous!" Bri screeches from my phone. Her voice is tinny and far away, like she's calling me from a soup can or something. How can Bri be in a soup can? My head hurts. I think I'm gonna faint.

"I have to delete this." My voice also sounds funny, like it's not coming from me.

"No way!" Bri stops me. "You're famous! And so is Kevin! I bet you'll get to be on TV and everything."

"No, you don't understand. Mom is gonna *kill* me if she finds out."

"Oh." Her joking tone is immediately replaced with seriousness. I lean against my wall, already feeling a little better. Bri won't laugh this off. She'll help me. "You're right. Your mom *cannot* find out. Does she have Instagram?"

"No." Mom hates all social media and says it rots everyone's brains. The only thing she has on her phone is Candy

Crush, which is so old I'm surprised she hasn't beaten every level yet.

"Okay, that's good!" Bri sounds tentatively optimistic. "She probably won't see it, then. Unless you get super famous and people want you and Kevin to star in a show or something."

I'm hot and cold all over. All I can think of is angry Mom from this morning. She will definitely be disappointed if she sees this. And probably also kill me. "I'm deleting it right now."

"No, wait!" Bri cries. "Just give it a day, okay? Things will die down later by tomorrow, surely. Nothing stays popular forever. And honestly, you deserve it! You were so happy."

I frown at my phone. Maybe Bri's right. Instagram does make me pretty happy . . . and it is nice to see all the cat pictures people send. I look up as Kevin wanders into my room, stretching and licking his whiskers. He rubs his face on my calves and purrs, and my racing heart slows down. Bri is right. It's not a big deal; it's just one video that everyone will lose interest in soon.

I put my phone on my bed and use both hands to pick up Kevin. He purrs louder and rubs his face against mine.

"Okay," I tell Bri, Kevin, and myself. "Just one day. Everything will be back to normal tomorrow."

Everything is not back to normal.

As soon as I step into homeroom, I know it's bad. Everyone's heads swivel toward me like puppets pulled along on a string. I stop, wary of all the eyes, but everyone just keeps staring. Then, Kenny breaks the silence by bounding to me. He holds his hand up for a high five.

"Congrats on going viral, Nova!"

I blink at him. I've never spoken to Kenny in my entire life. We're nowhere close to real friends; he's not even an acquaintance. But because of the video, he's talking to me. He, and maybe everyone in the room, remembers I exist. A slow smile creeps onto my lips. I take a deep breath and slap my palm against his, so hard it hurts a little.

"Thanks, Kenny."

After that, my day is complete chaos. Everyone congratulates me all day, even some teachers! In science, Mrs. Warble shows the video to everyone on the projector. Normally, I'd be embarrassed to see myself yelling at Kevin in front of the whole class, but everyone laughed! And Kevin looks extra cute on the big screen. By the time I get to math, I'm floating on air.

"Hi, Mr. Wickett," I say before he has a chance to greet me. He gives me a small smile, which is the most positive emotion I've ever seen on his face.

"Hello, Miss Harris. Don't let the excitement of today throw you off course."

I can't help but grin back. Okay, it's just fifteen minutes of fame like Mom says, but it's been a *really* good fifteen minutes.

I sit in my chair and pull my homework from my backpack. It took me extra long to do last night because Bri and I giggled through every problem, but I'm sure it's right. It has to be—

Lily enters the room, and all thoughts of math and viral videos flee my head like a herd of stampeding elephants. She flashes me a brilliant smile, and I swear my heart starts beating triple time.

"Nova, I love your video!" Lily squeals as she sits next to me. "I didn't know you had a cat!"

I blink at her. I'm pretty sure my brain is happy mush. "His name is Kevin," I manage.

"God, that's such a cute name for a cat. How old is he? When did you get him? Tell me everything!"

I try to force my pile of heated mush to remember some Kevin facts, but I take too long and Mr. Wickett starts his math lesson. There's no way I can pay attention though, because Lily gently places her warm palm on my arm. I turn and she passes me a piece of paper. I scan it—

I want to hear all about Kevin! Will you sit with me, Kylie, and Raina at lunch today?

I stare at Lily, starstruck, and she smiles back. I think I might throw up from happiness. Lunch! With other people! And not just any other people, but with Lily! And the other popular girls who are equally pretty! Maybe even . . . real friends? Not yet, but potentially the first step? And all because of Kevin the greedy cat and one doomed slice of pizza.

Bri was so right. I can never delete this video.

CHAPTER 4

I stand at the end of the lunch line, my hands slick around my orange lunch tray. I'm sure I'll throw up. Or faint. Or both. In front of everyone! Then someone will take a video of me and post it on their Instagram, and that'll replace my viral video of Kevin.

I shudder at the thought as I punch in my lunch number. I have to stay conscious, at the bare minimum.

I turn away from the lunch line and I don't even have time to debate where to sit. Normally I go to the last table on the left, where no one sits, but today, Lily waves at me from the table right in the middle of the room. The table where she, Kylie, and Raina sit—next to *eighth* graders, because they're that cool.

"Nova!" Lily calls, like I can't see her cute self waving frantically at me. "Over here!"

I take a shaky breath and channel Kevin. He wouldn't let a little fear of really cute, really popular girls get between him and lunch. In fact, he would tackle them to the ground if it meant getting an extra treat. I end up smiling at the thought, and at Lily, and somehow that convinces me to unstick my tennis shoes from the greasy tile and sit right next to the cutest girl I've ever met.

"I'm so glad you made it!" Lily says. She's squealing again, like in math, happiness lighting up her face like a million fireflies. I'm so stunned, I can't even stammer out a reply.

"Hi, Nova," Kylie says, and I reluctantly look away from my own personal sun. She's smiling just as brilliantly as Lily, but I don't feel dazzled like I do when Lily smiles. "*Love* your video. Your cat is the best! And his name is Kevin? Love it when cats have human names."

"Hey," Raina grunts. She's leaning on one hand, eyes half closed like she's bored. Fear seizes my heart—is she bored of me? Already?! I just sat down! But then she adjusts her hand, and her bracelets slip into view. They're handmade, and all the colorful beads are shaped like cats. She nods at me. "Cool cat."

I'm still speechless. I can't believe this is happening. That I'm sitting here! Kylie is talkative and Raina cool and aloof (extra ten points on my vocab quiz this week, Mrs. Paulson), and Lily is *Lily*. Lily Weston, coolest and cutest girl at Meadowbrooke Junior High. And they're all letting me hang out with them because of Kevin. He's getting so many snacks when I get home.

I can't mess this up like I mess up everything else. I can't be too weird or too quiet. I have to be exactly what they want, because this is my chance at making real friends. Maybe my only chance because everyone has established friend groups already. Even though I'll be at the private school next year (for sure!), I still have the rest of this year. And it sucks having no friends! I want a Tiffany and Skylar and cool lunches and Lily looking at me with interest instead of just being polite because we sit together in math. No, I have to be perfect this time, and not mess it up like with Mom and the private school exam. Kevin gave me a priceless, once-in-a-lifetime chance, and I can't waste it. I take a deep breath, sucking in my nerves and awe and replacing it with fearless, very-much-normal steel.

"Thanks for letting me sit here." My voice comes out normal, not shaky at all. Yes!

"Of course," Lily says, her voice warm. "You can always sit with us. Where'd you sit before?"

The truth sticks on my tongue. *In the very back of the lunchroom where no one could see me* isn't a cool response. Maybe I can bend the truth, just a little. For the sake of making new friends. I have to make a good first impression, right? "In the library. I like to, uh, read while I eat."

"Wow," Kylie says, and she really does sound impressed. "That's why you're so smart, huh?"

She thinks I'm smart too? Like Lily said? My face fills with flattered heat, but I don't get to say anything else because Kylie keeps talking.

"God, I'm starving. I'm so glad Mom packed sausage balls! They're left over from my parents' fancy party, y'all know the one. Oh, Nova, you don't, but it's not exciting at all, just boring adults drinking wine and stuff. They have them all the time; it's so annoying. Wait, are you only eating a salad?" Kylie asks.

I blink, trying to decipher the barrage of information. "What?"

Raina nods at my salad. I'm just now noticing she has a lunch in a familiar cutesy box. Ugh, not a bento box! I try to hold in my dismay when she reveals octopus-shaped hotdogs and veggie stir-fry. "Your salad. Are you on a diet?"

My armpits feel prickly and hot all of a sudden. I'm not on a diet. Mom says diets are for people who hate carbs and themselves. I don't know if that's right, but I don't think I need to be on a diet. Do I? For the first time, I'm scrambling to think about how my body looks to them. Should I say I am? It's better than saying "I'm a vegetarian." They might think I'm weird and not want to be friends. I weigh the options of weird and a liar, and I pick the liar.

"Umm, yes. I am."

Lily gets really still beside me. Like someone froze her with a freeze ray. She looks away from her delicious-looking spaghetti and my stomach drops to my toes. For some reason, I feel like I chose wrong. I shouldn't have said that. I shouldn't have lied.

Kylie glances at Lily, worry crossing her face, but Raina nods with approval. "Same. Mom is constantly on my case about eating too much."

That's weird. Why would her mom tell her to stop eating? Her bento box looks like a normal portion to me. I frown, but something tells me I shouldn't poke at that just yet. That's a best friend topic, probably. "Well, if you get hungry, you can have some of my salad anytime."

Raina chuckles and Lily finally starts moving. She says, her voice soft, "And my spaghetti. But you know that."

"I'd love some spaghetti," I say without thinking. No, my diet lie!

Kylie giggles. "Must be cheat day, huh?"

I shrug apologetically. "You caught me."

38

"What are your cheat days?" Raina asks. "We'll bring you snacks."

I glance at Lily. She still looks guarded but a little more relaxed. Not frozen solid like before. But I don't want her to be sad. I hate that she's sad because I lied and couldn't tell her I'm a vegetarian, just like I can't tell Mom. I hate that I hurt her because I can't be brave. Even when I should. So I lean in close and say, "I'll tell you a secret—every day is cheat day."

Lily finally smiles, right at me, and Kylie and Raina laugh, and I think this may be the start of something really amazing.

CHAPTER 5

"Oh, something is *definitely* up," Bri says in my ear, distrust dripping from her tone.

I'm home from school now, trying to recover from the best and weirdest day of middle school I've ever had. I need to do some exam practice, but I just came right up to my room and called Bri. I'm lying on my bed with all my limbs stretched out. Mom calls this my "thinking position." I don't know if I think better like this, but I hope so. There's a lot to think about. Bri-the-phone is on speaker, resting on my stomach with the bottom pointed to my face.

"I don't know, Bri, they seem nice."

"Yeah, sure." Bri's voice is staticky and sarcastic. "Let's start being nice *right* when Nova is super famous and popular."

My eyebrows pull together with worry. When she says it like that . . . but no. That doesn't mean anything. They're potentially my new friends, so I should treat them like they're already friends, right? And you have to believe in your friends and that they're not using you for nefarious (extra points again!) purposes.

"No way. They like me."

"They like the you that's on a *diet*." I can practically see Bri rolling her eyes. "Where'd that come from, anyway? I've never heard you even mention a diet."

"Raina asked," I argue.

"And you couldn't just say you like salad?"

"What normal person likes salad?"

"That's fair," Bri concedes. "But you do! You should have just said that."

I groan and scrub my face with my hands. "It's not the salad."

41

"Ah!" Bri says. "It's that you're a vegetarian, right?"

I nod, even though she can't see me. She must imagine that I am, though, because she keeps talking.

"What's wrong with being a vegetarian? You care about the environment and cute fuzzy animals!"

"So do you," I counter, "but you still eat the cute fuzzy animals."

"No way. I only eat the ugly ones."

I giggle and Bri does too. We've had this same conversation a hundred times, ever since I decided the meat life wasn't for me. When I explained that I read greenhouse gases were destroying the ozone and the meat industry is cruel and unsustainable, Bri rolled her eyes and swapped out the beef stir-fry she made for a tofu one. She doesn't care, even if she teases me. We have these familiar, comforting fake arguments all the time. I know Bri loves me, no matter what. But I don't ever bring up how when I told her mom I couldn't eat the taquitos she made from scratch, she made a face at me like I was an annoying mosquito. Like she'd rather squash me than make

42

anything else. And when I think of Mom or Lily making that same face, I want to crawl into bed and hide forever. And that's why I will only ever have this fun, fake argument with Bri and no one else.

"Okay, fine," Bri says after she catches her breath. "You're on a diet and what else? You like country music too?"

"Don't insult me with country music," I say, unable to hide my disgust. This sends Bri into a fresh fit of giggles, and I try to hold back my laughter too. "But no, that's it. Just the diet thing and then I kinda backed out of that. No big deal!"

"Nova Harris, when have your lies never been a big deal?" Bri's laughing while she scolds me. I laugh too, and it takes me a second to realize Bri's fallen silent. "Seriously, be careful, okay? I know Lily is the love of your life and can do no wrong, but I don't remember Raina and Kylie being particularly nice people."

My eyebrows pull together with worry, but also annoyance. Bri's never even talked to them! What does she know about them? Less than me. "They're good people. I can just tell."

"I mean, you say that, but—"

"Why do you get to have new friends and I don't?"

Bri and I are both silent. I didn't mean to say that! It just slipped out. I rub my hands over my face and grit my teeth. I can't have Bri being mad at me too. She's right; they're not my friends, not yet. Bri's my best friend.

"Bri, I'm sorry—"

"No, you're right." I wince, trying to read Bri's tone. She doesn't sound angry, but I can't see her face. Once again, I find myself wishing I could talk to her in person about this. "I'm not giving them a chance. They can't be too bad if Lily hangs out with them, right?"

"Right." I can't hide the relief in my voice. She's not mad and she sees what I mean. Thank goodness.

I hear a muffled sound of another voice, and Bri says "what?!" in Spanish. She says a few more words, and I manage to catch "minute" and "dinner." I glance at Kevin, who's snoozing in my closet, as usual. Good thing he isn't bilingual.

"Gotta go, Nova," Bri says.

I push down the sadness and smile at my ceiling. "Okay. Talk tomorrow?"

"You know it! And hey, listen. I love that you're a vegetarian and a weirdo who likes salad and those metal songs where they're screaming instead of singing. And people who don't like that don't deserve to be your friend."

I blink at the ceiling, wishing I could believe her. "Okay."

"Ugh, you're impossible! Bye!"

I laugh. "Bye, Bri."

When Bri hangs up, I continue staring at the ceiling, trying to think. I want to believe Bri, but I can't. I can't take anyone looking down on me like her mom did. I shudder and close my eyes. It's not so bad, the lying. I'm still me! Just . . . a little altered. A little shinier. Palatable! Yes, that's a good one. I could write the vocab quizzes for Mrs. Paulson.

Soon, I get tired of staring, so I sit up. My eyes dance with little black dots for a second, but soon they're gone, and I hop off my bed. I stretch and throw my hands into the air, which scares Kevin out of his nap.

"Sorry, Kev." I lower my arms as he waddles to me, already purring. I pat his soft fur as he rubs against my legs. "It'll be fine, right? New friends? Bri says they might be using me, but the video won't be popular for long. So I guess we'll see." A hollow kind of sadness fills my gut at the thought. I'll be so sad if Bri's right. But at least I got to sit with them for one day. That's something, right? I nod to myself and sit at my desk to start tonight's exam prep, but I can't really convince myself to believe it.

CHAPTER 6

I think I might have a problem. Scratch that—I have several problems.

I thought the video would die out, like they usually do, but it's been a few days and not a lot has changed. And there hasn't been a huge number of views like the first day, but my new followers have stuck around. There are *twenty thousand* of them. I can't even think of a number that big! I still have so many comments and DMs, I can't even look through them all. People are commenting on my old pictures too, saying how cute Kevin is but also wanting to see more. I'm really overwhelmed. Which is bad, because I need to do my exam prep like normal, but I have to do something about all these people who want to look at Kevin. I can't quit right when I finally might have real friends, and they want to see Kevin too.

"Kevin!" I call. I wander through the living room, peeking under the couch and armchair. Normally he would come running when I call, but I swear he can tell when I have my phone out. I don't want to torture him, but I have to have something for Instagram . . .

I give up calling and grab a bag of treats from under the sink. I shake them, just once, and Kevin barrels down the stairs, already screaming. I grin at him as he winds around my legs, mouth wide open in hopes I'll drop some treats and he can catch them.

"I love you, Kev," I say, laughing, as I take a bunch of pictures with my phone. My socks are in most of them, but you can't really see them because of Kevin's huge body blocking the way. Mission success! I give him two treats and he purrs, rubbing his face against my legs.

I put the treats away and go to the couch to edit the pictures I took. Kevin follows me and hops onto the couch too, settling next to me and tucking his paws under him like a distinguished Victorian gentleman. I laugh and try to take a picture, but he turns his head and growls.

"Okay, sorry," I say, smiling. "Picture time is over." I turn my attention to my phone and my smile fades. It's already 3:30 . . . when am I gonna have time to study? I groan when I remember I have to read some chapters of another sad dog book. I love reading, but not really for school. I always feel like I'm missing something, and Mrs. Paulson will add some random detail to our pop quizzes. So it takes me forever to finish books. With the extra exam prep, I'll probably be up late again tonight. But I can't oversleep again, no matter what . . .

I shake my head. Instagram first, then I can start reading. I finish editing and quickly post a picture of Kevin, mouth open mid-yowl, and add the caption "feed me!" I include some hashtags, and I'm done. I start to scroll to Bri's Instagram, but a red notification pops up at the top of the screen. And then . . .

another. And another! I watch people like Kevin's photo, one after another until it's up to five hundred likes in just ten minutes.

"Kevin," I whisper, my voice hushed with awe, "you really are famous." He just yawns in response. Even if he could understand being famous, I don't think he'd care. Unless all his new followers mailed him food.

Comments pop up under the new picture almost as fast as the likes.

WillieWhale: He's so cute!

DaisyH: My cat is just like that

TrevorKnowles76: well feed him already lol

I can't stop grinning at my phone. There are so many people now! I try to click on their profiles, but I don't recognize anyone. WillieWhale is all the way from Canada! I keep reading, fascinated.

CatFriend45678: I LOVE HIM LET ME HOLD HIM PLEASE

DoreenWhite: His coat is dull and he looks scruffy. Are you feeding him right or just snacks?

Whoa, wait a minute. Scruffy? What?! I glance at Kevin, who's rolled on his back and snoring. He doesn't look scruffy to me. Maybe his fur is dull? Maybe she means his teeth are yellow? But he's an old cat, so that's normal . . . isn't it? I leave Instagram and spend ten minutes googling how old cats should look, but I don't find anything useful. Should I take him to a vet? Mom would be mad, but if he looks scruffy . . .

I go back to Instagram to ask Doreen what she means, but there are so many comments now, it's hard to find her comment again. And then I stop short, because I have a comment from an Instagram account I know well.

LilyWeston23: I love Kevin so much!! He's so cute!! Also I love your socks :)

My head is fuzzy with glee. Lily commented on my picture! LILY FOLLOWS ME ON INSTAGRAM! I didn't even know she followed me! I must have missed it when the avalanche of new people came in. And she loves my socks! I glance down at my pink-and-orange polka-dotted socks like I've never seen them before. How do I reply?! My face and neck are hot and sweaty (man, I'm always sweaty now), and I let out a high-pitched squeal of happiness. Kevin rolls to his side and glares at me with one eye.

"What do I say, Kevin?!"

Kevin grunts and curls into a ball. No help from him. Wait, Bri! I leave Instagram and send a hurried text to her, complete with a screenshot of Lily's comment. I watch for the text bubbles anxiously. For a minute . . . two . . . five. No bubbles. She didn't see it.

My excitement cools and gets replaced by sadness and a little bit of annoyance. She's always on her phone! Is she ignoring me? To hang out with Tiffany and her bento boxes, I'm sure.

The thought of Tiffany makes my stomach sour, but it snaps me back to reality too. What am I doing? I shouldn't be messing around with Instagram and googling old-man cats and even Lily and her excellent taste in socks. I need to be *studying*. I can't get distracted. I gasp when I see the time: 4:30! I lost a whole hour and a half doing nothing since I got home! I groan and hop off the couch, leaving my phone behind. I pick up Kevin instead, ignoring his sleepy grumbles as I cart him upstairs.

"Come on, Kev. Homework time."

I study hard, only pausing for dinner, and I'm proud that I finish all the tasks on my to-do list before midnight. Everything will be fine, if I can just stay focused. Instagram is exciting, but I can't let it take over my life because it's not nearly the most important thing. Getting into private school is important. Making Mom proud is important.

Still, late that night, I think about Lily's comment and grin into the dark until I fall asleep. Maybe she can be important too.

CHAPTER 7

I sit down next to Lily for the third time in a row at lunch. She smiles at me, a slow, shy one that makes my heart start tap-dancing in my chest.

"Salad again?" she asks, nodding at my plate.

I hold in a sigh. Meadowbrooke Junior High really isn't good at vegetarian options. Sometimes I eat salad for lunch ten days in a row. But I can't tell Lily that, so I smile back and say, "Yeah, but I don't mind. I try to change up my salad dressings."

"Nova, that's the saddest thing I've ever heard," Kylie says. She collapses into her chair, heaving out the sigh I'm holding in.

"Anyway, can y'all believe the homework Mr. Wickett assigns? I'm dying."

"Me too," I admit. This isn't a lie. Every time I think I've gotten the hang of it, Mr. Wickett assigns something even harder. It's like trying to catch a slippery eel with your bare hands. Lily grimaces in solidarity, so that's three of us. Hope flutters in my chest. Maybe it's not weird that I'm struggling. Maybe it's just a really hard class.

"I get it," Raina says. She takes a delicate bite out of her cute box. Today's is a black tin with chalklike designs on the sides, and ham and cheese crackers, grapes, and cookies. Which would be fine, except the cookies are shaped like Hello Kitty, and the cheese is cut into the shape of bows. I glare at the box like I can curse Tiffany from afar.

"That's because you're a math genius," Kylie complains, bringing me back to the conversation. My stomach does uncomfortable, anxious flips. I agreed too early. I should have waited for Raina's response.

Lily perks up at my side. She smiles at me, her gaze warm

and friendly. "Don't mind Raina, Nova. She's a math genius, but you're an all-around genius."

"Which is way better," Kylie cuts in. Raina nods seriously, like she's not even mad. Maybe she agrees! Warm heat fills my face. I think I'm embarrassed, but I also feel sort of warm and gooey in my belly. They sound like Bri. As the warmth spreads to my chest, I realize that it's something a real friend would say.

We eat and chat for a few minutes, and then Lily speaks to Raina. "Do you have tennis practice today? I was thinking we can—"

"I don't think I'm taking tennis anymore," Raina says. Lily stiffens in surprise and Kylie does too. Raina still looks bored.

"Why?" Kylie asks.

Raina shrugs, but I notice she's not looking them in the eye. She's staring at her half-eaten cheese bows. "I've been off my game lately. I get too tired."

No one says anything for a second. Is it weird to want to quit tennis because you don't like it anymore? I've never been into sports or anything, really. Bri plays piano but she hates it, and I've always been too busy studying. Kylie and Lily exchange glances, and they look worried. Raina just seems kind of sad. I clear my throat. "I don't like tennis either. Too much running."

Raina looks up at me and half smiles. I smile back as Kylie laughs.

"Nova, you crack me up. Oh, that reminds me . . ." Kylie digs in her lunch box and withdraws the cutest little tin with hearts and fancy white trim on the lid. She gives it to me, and I take it; it's hot against my fingertips. Curiosity stirs in my chest. What is it? A gift? But what gift is hot? I open the tin and the warm feeling of friendship disappears. Inside are three, perfectly round . . .

Meatballs.

No. Oh no. I have to work really, really hard not to let the discomfort show on my face.

Kylie doesn't seem to notice. She grins at me, absolutely beaming. "I can't watch you eat salad every day, it depresses me. I already have to listen to Raina complain about liquid diets."

"Protein shakes are good for you," Raina drones in a nasally voice, maybe imitating her mom.

Kylie rolls her eyes. "*Anyway*, I asked Mom if she'll make me a few extra of everything when she makes my lunch! She's a really good cook, like almost a chef."

I'm nodding, but I'm feeling the prickly beginnings of sweat in my armpits. How am I going to hide this?! Meatballs are the absolute *worst*. They're just a big hunk of meat, sometimes corpses of cows *and* pigs! A corpse ball of mixed-up animals! It makes me so sad and also terribly ill. I can't eat this. There's no way.

But I can't let them know I'm a vegetarian either. We're almost real friends; I can't mess this up. Kylie is still grinning, waiting for my response, and Lily is watching me really closely for some reason. She has Laser Eyes, like Mom.

"Do you like meatballs, Nova?" Lily asks. She's looking at me so much! I'm gonna die!

"Oh, for sure." The lie doesn't come as easily as usual. It

sticks in my throat, like a glob of peanut butter. "But I'm not hungry yet. My salad is pretty filling."

"Sure," Kylie says. "But don't save them for too long! They'll go bad."

"Right," I say, because her words make perfect sense. Of course I should eat them before they spoil. She even warmed them up for me. But my brain is screeching at the word *eat*, and I think I've maybe short-circuited because before I know it, the lunch bell rings and it's just me and these three perfect meatballs my new-maybe-friend asked her mom to make for me that I can't eat.

Kylie and Raina wave as they head to science class. I wave back, and then I bolt to my old sitting place. There's a trash can right beside where I sit, hidden behind a corner. That's why no one wants to sit there; the smell gets pretty gnarly sometimes. I've gotten pretty good at blocking the scent out, but I always wished I had somewhere less smelly to sit. But today, this little corner is my salvation. I sneak into the corner and open the cute tin.

"Sorry, dead cows and or dead pigs," I whisper, and then I dump the contents of the tin into the trash. The three meatballs land on top of someone's half-eaten pizza, bouncing like basketballs until they settle into the mushy garbage, and I've never felt so relieved in my life.

"You could have told her you didn't want them, you know."

I freeze. No. No way . . . ! I watched Raina and Kylie leave! But this isn't either of their voices. It's the voice I know the best because I hear it every day in math and also in my daydreams. I turn, lead in my belly, and meet the eyes of Lily.

She has her arms folded, one eyebrow lifted in surprise. My brain immediately panics—she's gonna dump me! As a friend, because we're not girlfriends! We're not even friends really, actually! My brain scrambles to work through the terror of getting caught and finding the right thing to say, but all my thoughts are mixed up and full of fear. My face fills with panicked heat, and I suddenly want to flee the cafeteria and school and maybe my whole life.

"I . . ." I can't think of anything to say. The reality is settling in now—Lily caught me in a lie. She caught me. No one has ever caught me before. I always tell Bri the truth (eventually) and I always avoid Mom's Laser Eyes. This is the first time something like this has happened, and I'm not prepared for how to deal with it.

Lily doesn't seem mad. She just looks curious. "It's okay if you don't like meatballs. You can just tell Kylie."

I shake my head before I know what I'm doing. I can't think of a way to cover this up. She caught me red-handed.

"You don't want to hurt her feelings?" Lily asks.

Yes. Yes! That's it. "Yeah," I finally manage. My brain quickly wraps around the lie and I make it my own. "Kylie's really nice, and I don't want to be rude." And it has nothing to do with being a vegetarian at all.

Lily smiles. "You won't offend her. Maybe you can ask for something specific if you don't like meatballs. So you don't have to pretend to like salad every day."

"No, I really do like salad." I blink. I told Lily the truth without even thinking. Bri said people who like salad are weird; will Lily think so too? I feel like I'm going to throw up.

But Lily doesn't make fun of me. She laughs and stands right next to me. "Okay, Nova. I'll make you a deal. I won't tell Kylie about the meatballs if you promise me something."

"What?"

"I want you to promise that you won't lie to me."

I stare at Lily, an uneasy feeling crawling over my skin. That's hard. That's really, really hard. What if she doesn't like me? What if she thinks the real Nova is lame and she doesn't want to be my friend? But Lily is looking at me, so kindly. And she didn't get mad that I threw the meatballs away. Maybe I can try. Maybe it'll work out.

I stick my hand out, and Lily seems surprised. But a second later, she completes the handshake. Her hand is warm and a little rough to the touch.

"Deal," I say. I don't know why, but I'm feeling really serious.

And like maybe this isn't a bad idea, even if my brain is doubtful.

Lily squeezes my hand, and everything except a pleasant shiver flees my body. "Deal. I really look forward to getting to know you, Nova."

CHAPTER 8

"Bri, you don't understand. She TOUCHED MY HAND."

Bri's laughter crackles over the phone. "You are so gay, I can't deal."

"No, listen. It was amazing. Her hand wasn't soft! Isn't that cool? Do you think she, like, practices fencing or something?"

"I'm hanging up," Bri threatens, but she's still laughing.

I grin at the ceiling. I'm home now, but I can't focus on exam prep or homework. I struggled for an hour but caved and called Bri instead because I can't hold this in. Lily Weston touched my hand! And said she wanted to get to know me! And didn't snitch on me to Kylie, who is clearly one of her best friends! This is true happiness.

"I wanna know more about this deal," Bri says. My smile fades into a frown. "Are you gonna keep it?"

"I'm going to try." That's what I say, but even I hear the doubt in my voice.

"Yeah, right." Bri snorts. "You shouldn't have said that. It'll hurt worse now if she catches you lying, because you promised you wouldn't."

"I know," I groan. I roll around on my bed, and Kevin lifts his head in alarm. He hisses grumpily and moves to snooze on top of my pillow. "You weren't there! I was all sweaty and my heart was going to jump out of my chest and I just said okay without thinking."

"Sounds like what someone in love would say," Bri teases.

"Leave me alone," I groan. "You don't get it. You didn't have the weird puberty."

"I think the only weird part is you thinking of being gay as 'weird puberty.'" Bri laughs. "But you're right, the crush part is pretty weird. Tiffany talked my ear off all day about how hot Aaron Jennings is. But last month, we all agreed he's a meathead and a jerk."

Ugh. Tiffany, my one-sided enemy. I bet she did talk about her crush all day and eat her nauseatingly cute homemade lunch at the same time. And I bet Bri listened, when she didn't even respond to my sock crisis until an hour later, and then it was too late to answer Lily. "Of course she did," I mutter under my breath.

"What?"

"What? Nothing. How was piano today?"

Bri's quiet for a second and I wince. I can practically see her eyes narrowing. "Nova, is there something you wanna talk about—"

I hear heavy footsteps outside my room. Panic fills my chest, and I sit up and hang up the phone in one motion. Sorry, Bri— can't get caught slacking off. A second later, Mom opens my door wide.

Mom's still in her work clothes, a nice black-and-white flowy shirt, zebra-striped earrings I got her for Christmas, and black pants, so she must have just gotten home. She's not smiling. "Sounds like a party in here."

I swallow the lump in my throat. I'm in trouble. I was supposed to be doing my homework. I glance at the time on my phone and nearly groan out loud. How is it five o'clock already?! I can't keep up with everything lately. "I know. I was just taking a break."

Mom makes a "hmm" sound, but she gets distracted when Kevin jumps off my bed and rubs against her legs. "Come on, cat, stop that." Kevin doesn't listen and just purrs. Mom isn't a cat person; she's never even picked up a cat before. But still, she leans over and rubs Kevin's head for a moment. When she straightens, she doesn't seem that mad anymore. Thank you, Kevin!

"You know it's homework time before phone time," Mom says, but there's no bite to her voice anymore.

"I know. I'm sorry."

I hold my phone in a tight fist, praying she doesn't take it.

But she doesn't. Instead, she motions for me to come closer. "I got off early today, so I picked up d—" Mom stops herself before she says the forbidden word. Kevin looks up at her, his cute little ears perked and ready. "I picked up . . . sustenance."

I giggle and Mom finally smiles. "What kind of sustenance?"

"Chinese food."

Oh yay! I always get veggie lo mein, even before I quit eating meat. A meal I don't have to pretend I like or sneak the meat to Kevin under the table while she's not looking. Perfect! I hop off the bed and skip to Mom. She surprises me with a one-armed hug.

"Come on, let's eat."

Kevin immediately starts yowling and runs downstairs as fast as he can. Mom sighs with her whole body. "Guess we have to ban 'eat' now too."

I laugh and hug her back with both my arms. I hope she isn't too mad at him, but she seems like she's in a good mood today. No volcanoes!

After I lock Kevin in his baby cage (this time with my

backpack as a weight on top), Mom and I eat our food. Mom tells me about her day, and I tell her about mine (leaving out the meatball fiasco, Lily's deal, and the fact we started a new unit I don't get in math . . . I didn't have a lot to say). When we're done, and all the leftovers are put away, Mom gets her laptop out. I watch her out of the corner of my eye while I rinse out Kylie's pretty tin in the sink. Mom yawns, but then she stretches her arms to the sky and starts typing.

Mom is my hero. I know it's kind of lame for a twelve-year-old to say that, but I really mean it. She's so smart, and she's so tough. When I was a baby, she worked three jobs to support us. Not that I remember, but my old neighbor used to tell me about it all the time. And now Mom's going to college online, after she works all day! She's amazing. I miss hanging out with her; since she's always working and studying, we don't get to have movie nights or eat at Waffle House for breakfast for dinner anymore. And she gets mad easier, and Kevin irritates her more. But she said that once she finishes her degree, she'll get a huge pay raise at work, so I really don't want to bother her.

"What's wrong?" Mom looks at me, and I look to the floor. Dang it, I stared at her too long. I shake Kylie's tin free of water and turn it upside down to dry while I think of an answer. I miss her, but I can't tell her that. I don't want her to feel guilty.

"Nothing. But I was thinking . . ." I hesitate, but then take a deep breath and ask anyway. "Can I do my homework with you?"

Mom seems surprised. Then she smiles, a big, real one I haven't seen in almost a year. "Sure. Go get your books."

Warmth fills my whole body and I run to Kevin's cage to grab my backpack. He springs out as soon as I lift the bag and runs to the table to sniff around for stray crumbs. I pat his head and slide into the seat next to Mom.

"What're you working on?" Mom asks, looking over at my books.

"I have to read some for English, do some worksheets for science and history, and then my math stuff." I hope she doesn't ask about the math. If she asks what we're learning, I really have no idea.

But Mom just nods. "Good. Let's get started. I'll play some

70

music for us, huh?" Mom takes out her headphones and the computer starts blaring oldies. I complain and Mom laughs, and this is maybe the best night I've had in a long time.

A whole hour passes while I do my work. English, history, and science go by quickly, but then I'm left with math. Ugh. I tap my foot in time with Destiny's Child, but I don't feel any more relaxed. I hate math. I imagine Mr. Wickett's math sharks eating my foot. My hand twitches with the urge to draw the scene. Maybe a tiny picture won't hurt . . . I use the space next to a problem to draw a tiny shark with huge, gleaming teeth.

"You okay?" Mom startles me by asking. She turns down the music and inspects my nearly empty worksheet. Uncomfortable heat rises to my neck as she examines it. She's got the Laser Eyes again.

"I'm okay." I hope I sound confident. "Just taking a break."

Mom nods. "You've earned that. But if you get stuck, let me know, okay?"

"Okay," I say, even though I'm already stuck and I'd never let her know that.

She smiles and taps my doodle of the math shark. "Less of this and more numbers though, right?"

Mom laughs, but I don't. I want to sink down into my chair. I'm messing up *again*. I shouldn't be doodling; I should be working! I'm really tired, especially since I didn't sleep a lot last night, but I have to push through. I still have to do exam prep to make up for chatting with Bri earlier, and I can't do that in front of Mom.

"Sorry," I say, and throw myself into the next problem. Even if I don't understand now, I *will* understand. I have to. Because if I don't, I'll let Mom down. And that's not an option.

I work through seven more songs before I'm finally victorious. I admire my completed worksheet, something like joy in my heart. Take that, math sharks! I imagine myself punching one right in its big dumb nose.

"Good job," Mom says. She closes her laptop and yawns. "We're both done."

"You did a good job too," I tell her, and her expression softens. She kisses me on the top of my head.

"The Harris girls always get things done."

I smile back. Always. And that includes math, so I better get that done too. Mom works so hard, and I want her to be proud of me, like she is now. I don't want her to worry. And maybe, if I work as hard as she does, I'll make up for not being smart enough to get into private school the first time. So I'll defeat math once and for all, and I won't tell Mom anything that stresses her out, which definitely includes Instagram, my new friends, and being a vegetarian. Mom deserves to see the best, shiny version of Nova because she's right; the Harris girls get things done, no matter what. Failure is not an option.

CHAPTER 9

I sit down at the popular lunch table again. I keep thinking they'll get tired of me and kick me back to my lonely table by the garbage, but it hasn't happened yet. I can't believe it, honestly.

"Hey, Nova!" Lily smiles at me and I smile back. I've gotten a bit used to her sunshine smile, but only a little. My heart still can't act right when she looks directly in my eyes. It's a problem. A really nice problem I definitely want to have, but still.

"Hi." I can't help but look away as my face heats up. Ugh, I'm being so weird! I've really got to rein this in. I try to arrange my face into a normal expression, but I can't tell if it's working.

"Hello, hello," Kylie sings as she sits down. She zeroes in on my lunch, which I'm noticing is her sort of annoying habit. "Whoa, no salad today?"

I look down too. I only had to suffer a four-day salad streak this time. Today, the cafeteria had mashed potatoes, asparagus, and a really good-looking chocolate cake. "Yeah, I'm pretty excited about the cake."

"I would kill for some cake," Raina groans as she sits next to Kylie. Today, she brought a pink thermos with purple unicorns on it. I stare at it in disbelief. I thought Raina was *way* too cool for unicorns.

"I brought cookies," Lily says, unzipping her lunch box. "You can have one." She offers one to Raina, who eyes it like a lion looks at an injured gazelle.

"No, that's okay," Raina says finally. "My grandma pinched my stomach yesterday and said I was getting chubby."

A dark expression crosses Lily's face. She pulls back the cookie like she's been burned. When she speaks, it's with a tone I've never heard her use before. "Right. We don't want that."

Raina doesn't seem to react, but Kylie exchanges a worried glance with me. Whoa, what was that? I don't think I've ever seen Lily upset. No, not upset—she was *mad*. What's happening?

"Nova," Kylie says quickly. "I saw your new Instagram pictures! That cat is the cutest!"

I glance at Lily, but she's silent, still wearing a stormy expression on her face. I reluctantly look away and answer Kylie. "Yeah, he's a good cat. He doesn't really like pictures though, so I have to sneak them when he isn't looking."

"I'd love to see him," Raina says. She takes a delicate sip of the mystery liquid in her super cute thermos before she continues. "In person."

"Yeah!" Kylie looks like she's bouncing in her seat. "Can we come over today?"

Oh no. No way. Mom would have a *fit*. One of her rules is that I can't have strangers in the house unless she's there. I've only had Bri as a friend for years and Mom is best friends with Bri's mom, so it hasn't been an issue . . . until now. I fidget in my seat uneasily. What should I do? It's definitely uncool to refuse. They might not like me anymore if I say they can't see Kevin. He's a celebrity now, I guess; the last picture I posted got over five thousand likes, and it was blurry because he was running away from the camera! Of course they want to see him.

I'm startled when Lily puts a gentle hand on my arm. "You can say no."

"But you wouldn't," Kylie says, her voice full of hope. Raina's looking down at her phone, but she's scrolling aimlessly. Listening.

I sigh. Lily is kind, but I have to do this. I don't want to lose my seat at the lunch table. Obviously, I love being close to Lily, but now I kind of like Raina and Kylie too. I can't let them down.

"Okay. You can come. But!" I have to raise my voice over Kylie's excited squealing. "You have to be gone by five o'clock so my mom doesn't catch us."

"Deal!" Kylie looks like she's going to burst. Like a happy balloon. "I can't wait to meet him!"

We spend the rest of the lunch trading phone numbers (I can't believe I have Lily's number now!), and I text them all my address. My stomach does an uneasy lurch, but I stuff it down. It's okay, right? I mean, Mom just has that rule because she's big on safety. Kylie, Raina, and Lily wouldn't hurt me, so it's fine. And they're gonna be my real friends soon, so eventually she'd let them come over. I'm just being . . . proactive! Nothing to worry about.

Kylie and Raina leave the table a few minutes early to get to class before the bell, so it's just me and Lily. I start to get flustered, as usual, but some of the panic cools. Lily's staring after Raina, a complex mix of emotions on her face. She never did eat her cookies.

"If you're still offering," I say, "I want one of those cookies."

Lily looks at me in surprise. "But what about your diet?"

I hesitate. Oh man, I hate this part. No one ever finds out about my lies so I never have to come clean. But Lily was hurt, and I want to cheer her up. And I did promise to not lie to her. If we're going to be real friends, I should keep my promises.

"I lied. I'm not on a diet," I confess. It comes out all at once, in a rush. "In fact, I hate diets."

A slow smile spreads over her face. "Then why did you lie?"

"I thought that's what Raina wanted me to say." Shame heats up my face. "And I didn't want to have to admit I just really like salad."

Lily laughs. It's so loud and joyful, it blasts away all the icky shame and discomfort from telling the truth. "Thanks for telling me, Nova." She rummages in her lunch box and places a perfect chocolate chip cookie in my palm. "And you know what?"

I close my hand around the precious cookie I'm sure I'll never have the guts to eat. "What?"

Lily beams at me. "I like salad too."

CHAPTER 10

This was a terrible idea.

My stomach is twisted in terrible knots, and I'm sweaty again. I'm always sweaty these days. Curse you, weird puberty, and Mrs. Helen, for being right.

I stand vigil on my front porch, anxiously picking at the bottom of my shirt. They're not here yet, but I'm sure it'll be soon. I shouldn't have agreed to this. Horrible what-ifs play on repeat in my mind. Mom catching me. Kylie breaking something or Raina trying to kidnap Kevin. Kevin biting them and we have to go to the hospital for rabies or something. (Though he's definitely had his shots, so that one is unrealistic. The rest, though . . .) My stomach feels like I swallowed rocks. I have to call this off. Mom is gonna catch me, and she'll be so disappointed—

I squeal in terror when my phone buzzes, convinced Mom somehow heard my thoughts and is texting me. Or maybe it's Lily saying she changed her mind because I'm really lame and she doesn't even want to risk seeing my celebrity cat in case my uncoolness rubs off on her. I hate that my brain can't figure out what's worse.

I pull out my phone, but it's not Mom or Lily. It's Bri.

You're dead, Nova Harris. You are so dead.

I text her back several angry-frowny emojis. She responds right away.

What do you want me to wear to your funeral

I roll my eyes, but a small smile escapes my panic. Bri always knows what to say.

Anything but that awful Easter dress from last year

I told you to stop bringing that up!!!!

A giggle escapes and I'm only a little surprised (and terrified) when a dark car I don't recognize pulls into my driveway.

They're here.

Bri sends me a picture of her taking a selfie with her weenie dog, who looks like he's trying to bite her face. *Carl and I love you! Don't get caught!!*

I smile and put my phone away. I'm okay now. Bri is in my pocket, supporting me, and we have a whole hour and a half before Mom gets home. When Lily, Kylie, and Raina hop out of the car, I wave, and I don't even feel that nervous. Cool Nova is here.

A tall white lady leans out of the driver's side window and waves at me. Oh, I've seen her before—I think she's the local librarian! Is she Kylie's mom? "Hi, Nova!"

"Hi—" Oh no, what's her name? I search my brain, but I come up empty. "Umm, Kylie's mom?"

Kylie rolls her eyes and climbs my steps at lightning speed. "Bye, Mom, see you later, bye!"

"Love you!" Kylie's mom sings, laughing. "I'll be back to get you girls at four thirty, sharp. Can't stay out too late on a school night!"

"Okay," Lily says, smiling, and Raina nods. I wave a little and as soon as the car disappears, all the nerves rush back. It's really happening.

"I love your townhouse," Kylie gushes. "It's so cute! Cozy. Adorable."

"She means it's small," Raina drones. Lily gasps and Kylie stomps on her foot. Raina lets out a sound like a strangled chicken, and I can't help but laugh, even if Raina did call my house small.

"It's just me and Mom, so it's a good size for us."

"Exactly." Kylie shoots a poisonous glare at Raina, but Raina is staring down at her foot with tears in her eyes. Lily looks vaguely panicked and suddenly I am too. This isn't a good start! Why is everyone so tense?

"Want to see Kevin?" I ask before anyone can start arguing again.

"Yes!" Lily says. Kylie and Raina look up, eyes shining in eagerness. I breathe a sigh of relief and open my door.

"Kevin?" I call. He doesn't come to me right away—probably napping.

"Do you have a little sibling?" Lily asks from behind me. I turn in surprise and she's pointing to Kevin's baby jail.

"Oh no, that's for Kevin."

"He plays in a playpen?!" Kylie squeaks. "He's so cute I'm gonna die."

"No," I say, laughing. "Wait a minute, you'll see." I take a deep breath and cup my hands around my mouth. "Kevin, dinnertime!"

Footsteps thunder upstairs and then grow louder as Kevin comes barreling down the steps, yowling at the top of his lungs. He freezes for a second when he sees Lily, Kylie, and Raina but then ignores them as he launches himself into the kitchen to see what we have on the dining room table.

"Oh my God," Raina says, her jaw slack. "You have the perfect cat."

"He does this every day?!" Lily is laughing, and it's the best sound I've ever heard in my life.

"Yeah, but only if you say certain words," I admit as they crowd around the table. Kevin's eyes are huge, and his fur stands on end. "Oh, wait guys, let me feed him. He's not good with strangers."

Kylie reaches out to pet him anyway, but Lily smacks her hand. Kylie jumps, scowling, and Lily says, "Better me than him scratching you!"

"True," I say as I grab some treats from under the sink. Kevin jumps off the table and meows, rubbing his face against my legs. "I picked him up when I first met him, and he was not happy." I give them each a treat, and they bend down to Kevin's level. Kevin is shy around new people, but nothing is more important than food. He scoops up all three treats from their open palms, crunching happily.

"Where did you get him?" Lily asks. She's looking right at me, even as Kylie and Raina try to coax Kevin to them. He ignores their outstretched hands and cleans his face. I wish I had his confidence.

I rock back on my heels, a little frazzled. My brain doesn't know what to do. Should I lie? Is getting a cat from an expensive breeder cooler? Will they judge me for adopting him from my neighbor's porch? But I promised I wouldn't lie to Lily. Oh, what should I—

"It doesn't matter," Raina says. She's watching him like he's the most incredible thing she's seen in her whole life. Kevin just cleans his whiskers. "Look at him! He's perfect!"

"Will he pose with us?" Kylie asks me. "For Instagram?"

I frown. "I thought you just wanted to meet him?"

"We do!" Kylie says, but it's hasty and she's not looking at me. She hurries along. "He's really cute and I want to squeeze him!"

"He won't let you," I say, but my voice is hesitant. Something doesn't feel right. Is Kylie . . . lying? I stare at Kylie, frowning. "Why do you want him to pose with you?"

"No reason," Kylie says quickly. Again. "I just think it would be cool to have a picture of him! Like taking a picture with a famous person!"

"I can take your picture," I say slowly. My stomach is lead and heavy in my belly. Please don't let Bri be right. "I'll send it to you after."

"Great!" Kylie jumps to her feet and eases beside Kevin. He's so intent on cleaning his face, he doesn't see her. I raise my phone and take a really bad picture of her on purpose. When I send it, her face falls. "Oh no, take another one! We can't put that on Instagram!"

My face falls too. I didn't say I'd put her picture on Instagram. I thought they wanted to meet Kevin because they're my friends, but Bri was right. Kylie just wants to be on Kevin's Instagram so she can be more popular. I knew it. Well, Bri did. I was naive and now I'm hurt. They don't want to be my real friends at all.

"What's wrong?" Lily asks, moving to stand beside me. She reaches out a hand, but I step away. Even Lily can't make me feel better. I bet she doesn't like me at all, and I'm being stupid because of this stupid crush.

"Nothing," I lie, even though I promised her I wouldn't. She's lying to me, so what's the point? "Y'all can stand together, and I'll take your picture with him. I'll post it tonight."

Kylie squeals with joy and Raina joins her next to Kevin, but Lily doesn't move. I look at her, even though it's hard to meet her eyes. "Don't you want to be in the picture?"

Lily shakes her head. She's watching my face closely again, like she did at lunch when Kylie gave me the meatballs of death. She seems worried or maybe anxious. "I didn't come over to take pictures with Kevin."

"Oh." I blink at her, frowning. "Then why?"

"I wanted to hang out with you."

I blink again, this time in shock. Is she telling the truth? She can't be, right? Kylie and Raina are frozen, waiting for me to take the picture, but Lily is just watching me with an intense expression. Like she wants me to believe her.

Raina breaks the silence by standing. "I don't have to have

a picture either. Honestly, I just really like cats."

"Oh, same." Kylie stands too, but she looks disappointed. Kevin just cleans his whiskers, purring softly.

"Are you sure?" I'm asking Kylie and Raina, but I'm looking at Lily. And I only listen to her response when she says, "I'm sure." She touches my arm, and this time I let her. She smiles at me, and I slowly smile back. "Let's forget about the cat for now— sorry, Kevin. Let's hang out."

I'm not sure if I believe her, but I want to. I want to believe that Lily is here because she likes hanging out with me, that we're maybe real friends. And a secret part of me wants to believe that maybe she's here because she might like me.

"Okay." My voice is tentative but hopeful. "What do you want to do while we hang out?"

CHAPTER 11

When it's four thirty and Kylie's mom honks her car horn outside, we all groan.

"Already?!" Kylie sounds outraged. She throws down her playing cards grumpily. "Hold on, Nova, I'm gonna convince her to give us like ten more minutes so I can win this game!"

"No way," Raina says from my couch. She's texting on her phone. "My mom's already telling me to come home."

"Uugghh," Kylie growls. "Raina, come with me! Help me convince her!"

I watch as Kylie runs out of the house, and Raina trots slowly behind her.

I smile at Lily, and she giggles. Despite the rough start, I ended up having a lot of fun. I took them on a tour of my house, we ate some snacks, and we talked about how our gym teacher is marrying another gym teacher from another school. I think it's romantic, but Lily complained that since she got engaged, she only lets us play dodgeball, and Lily hates dodgeball. Kylie worries they will have an army of gym teacher children, and Raina didn't care because she finally got Kevin to lick her hand as he ate a treat and she said she was gonna die of happiness. We played cards and listened to music and it was just like a real hang out! Like I have real friends again.

But Bri's warning sat at the back of my mind the whole time, so I couldn't really relax around them, not completely. Kylie didn't bring up Instagram anymore, but I caught her staring longingly at Kevin a few times. I know Lily said she didn't care, but I don't know . . . I just don't want to be used.

It also doesn't feel good to hear Bri's "I told you so."

"Thanks for letting us hang out, Nova," Lily says. She looks right at me, a huge grin on her face, and despite feeling low, my heart speeds up. Before I know it, I'm all sweaty again. Lily will never like me! I'm the sweatiest person alive.

"Thanks for coming," I manage to squeak out.

"Do you think . . ." Lily suddenly seems shy. She fidgets with the sleeves on her shirt and won't look me in the eyes. I stare, fascinated. I've never seen her be shy before. She's confident, pretty, and amazing, but never shy. And definitely not weird like I am. "Do you think we could hang out again?"

At first, my heart sings with happiness. But then the gloominess over Kylie's and Raina's reactions returns, and I look at my feet. "I don't know, maybe."

"You didn't have fun?" Lily's voice makes me look up in alarm. She sounds so sad, and she looks sad too. Confusion and sadness cloud her face and I can't stand it. I hesitate but decide to tell her the truth.

"I did! And I'm glad everyone came over. But . . . I don't

know, my best friend told me that maybe y'all just wanted to be my friend because of Kevin. I didn't believe her, but Kylie . . ." I trail off.

Lily's face clears of confusion, but now she looks horrified. "Oh no, Nova! I promise, we just want to be your friend! I think you're really cool and I—" Lily stumbles over her words, and her eyes are wide with panic. "Honestly, I'm not even a cat person. I just wanted to hang out with you, but I thought it would be weird if I asked to come to your house for no reason."

I just stare at her for a second, dumbstruck. "Really?"

"Really. And . . ." Lily takes a deep breath, like she's hyping herself up. "And when I asked if you wanted to hang out, I really mean just us. Not that Kylie and Raina aren't cool, but . . ."

I stare at her for another dumbstruck second. Oh. Oh my God? Is this happening? Is this real?!

"You can say no." Lily's blushing! Her brown cheeks are turning a delicate red before my eyes. Oh my God.

"Yes!" The word is out of my mouth before I know it. "Yes, but not now! Mom will be back soon."

"Right, yeah, okay," Lily says quickly. "What about Saturday?"

I almost agree, but then I remember: This Saturday, I get to hang out with Bri. I only get to see Bri once every two weeks. I like Lily a lot, a whole lot after this afternoon, but I can't miss seeing Bri. But what do I say to Lily? I don't want to say no, but I have to, and she might be mad at me, and it'll ruin everything—

Lily startles me when she touches my arm. Her touch is light and unsure. "It's okay. You can tell me the truth."

I know I look distressed. My eyebrows have to be meeting in the middle. But I did promise I wouldn't lie . . . "I do want to hang out! But I was going to see my best friend on Saturday. So I don't want to cancel with her."

I wince, waiting for her to be mad, but it doesn't happen. Lily looks surprised and then . . . relieved? She gives me a big smile. "Oh, no problem! I don't want you to cancel with your friend! I can't hang out next weekend, though. I have practice."

Practice? For what? Wait, even worse—it has to be this

Saturday or nothing! I have to choose. Unless, I don't? "Wait, hold on." I text Bri a bright red SOS emoji.

Bri responds right away. *Did your mom catch you?? Are you dead????*

Not yet, I text back. *Can Lily hang out with us on Saturday?*

DID SHE ASK YOU ON A DATE????

My face is on fire. Lily is watching me too, so I know she can see it! Oh no, no, no—

NO she just wants to hang out Saturday. But I want to hang out with you too.

That's a date you idiot.

No it isn't! I'm sweating so much, ugh. *Can we all hang out? Please??*

Actually yes! Bri texts. *I'll be your wing girl.* Bri adds an emoji of a bird and an arm flexing. I breathe a sigh of relief.

"Lily," I say, really nervous, "do you want to hang out with me and Bri on Saturday?"

"Gabriella Torres?" Lily asks. I nod, stunned. She remembers

Bri? Wait, she remembers Bri is my best friend?! Lily smiles. "Yeah! She seems super cool! What're we doing?"

I'm so happy, I can't think. She said yes. She said yes!

"Lily!" Kylie calls, making us both jump. "Mom says we can't stay. Come on!"

"I'll text you," I say, and Lily nods, smiling.

"Okay. See you later! And Saturday!"

I wave and watch Lily leave my house. I wait for her to climb into Kylie's van and for them to drive away before letting out a screech of victory. Kevin narrows his eyes and presses his ears back in annoyance, but I can't stop. This has to be the best afternoon of my life! Mom would be terribly upset if she knew what I just did, and what I'm planning. But honestly, a volcano day might be worth it.

I'm really on a roll.

I had almost-friends at my house and they had a good time, I aced a pop quiz on *Where the Red Fern Grows*, and the best and most important of all—I have a date on Saturday! A date

Bri is also attending, but still! This has to be the best week of my life.

It only gets better when Mr. Wickett hands back our homework and I have a bright and shiny 90 written in red pen at the top of the page. I almost scream with glee. An A! Finally! Look out world—Nova Harris is coming through.

"Miss Harris," Mr. Wickett says as I pack up my stuff after class. "Can I see you for a second?"

My good mood is blasted away by fear. Oh no, was the A on my homework a mistake? Did I get someone else's grade? I approach his desk while everyone files out of the room. Lily frowns at me, and I try to smile back reassuringly, but I'm sure I look like I'm about to throw up. Because I am.

"Y-yes, sir?"

Mr. Wickett looks at me from behind his desk. His eyes are sharp, like Mom's Laser Eyes. Then, he does the impossible— he smiles!

"I wanted to tell you that you're doing a great job, Nova."

Whoa, what?! No way, is this really happening? Mr. Wickett

is so intense that lots of kids won't even take his class. He never says things like this! "Really?"

Mr. Wickett smiles even bigger. "Really. I can tell you work hard to understand the material. Even if you struggle with the homework, your progress is evident in your quizzes. I see your hard work."

Wow. Wow! I know I'm grinning like a dummy, but I can't help it. Mr. Wickett sees how hard I work. He sees that I stay up late every single night, and he sees that it's paying off. I can't ever be honest with Mom about how hard math is, but now I can be honest with Mr. Wickett. I think I might cry. That would be so embarrassing though, so I try to hold it in.

"Thank you," I manage. "I'm trying really hard."

"I know. I can tell. Do you have a tutor?" Mr. Wickett asks.

"No, sir." I feel my chest puff up, just a little. "I study really hard! Like almost two hours every night."

I thought he'd be proud, but Mr. Wickett's smile fades. "That's a long time to study, Miss Harris. Math is important but not at the expense of your health."

Oh. Well, now I don't know how to feel. I thought Mr. Wickett would be proud, like Mom is. But he seems . . . concerned? Anxiety creeps into the pride in my chest. Did I say something wrong? Should I not have told him how much I study?

"What do you think about getting a tutor?" Mr. Wickett asks. "I can set you up with one. Maybe if you see the work in a different way, it'll help you understand the material better."

A tutor . . . I don't think I'd mind a tutor. If I could do less math every day and still get good grades, that would be a major win. But then I'd have to tell Mom about it, because I'd have to stay late after school. Panic fills me all at once. She can't know I'm struggling.

"No thanks," I blurt. Mr. Wickett frowns so I keep talking. "I mean, I can do it by myself."

"There's no shame in getting a tutor. In fact, it shows you care about the material."

"No, I know, I just . . ." I search my brain frantically for a lie. "I want to prove to myself I can do it."

Mr. Wickett doesn't seem convinced, but he nods. "Okay.

But if you need help, you should feel encouraged to ask for it. You're doing a good job on your own, but I wanted to make it easier for you, if possible."

I nod, equal parts happy that he's trying to help and sick that I can't take it. I hate this! I wish, just once, I could be honest with Mom. But then everything would come out, and she'd find out just how much I've let her down. That would all but kill me.

"Thanks, Mr. Wickett."

"You're welcome, Miss Harris." He nods to the door. "Go on to your next class."

"Okay. See you tomorrow!" I wave and hurry from the room. I hope I'll calm down before I get to my next class but that sick, disappointed feeling lingers all day long.

CHAPTER 12

Mom pulls up to Deangelo Park at 9:55 a.m. Five minutes before I'm supposed to meet Bri.

And Lily.

I'm a mess. It took me forever to pick out my outfit. I ended up with a cute shirt, my best coat, and jeans, because what do you possibly wear to meet your crush? Not only was the choice impossible, but also I feel like none of my clothes fit me right anymore. I must have thrown three shirts in Kevin's clothes hoarding pile in frustration. This was in Mrs. Helen's puberty lesson too, but this is a really inconvenient time for it to show up! I'm in despair. I feel like I'm not cute enough for a first date with Lily and I just want to turn around and go back home. I'm having a terrible day already, and it hasn't even started yet!

"I'll be at the office," Mom says, breaking into my mental freak-out. I nod. Mom works at the bank right across the street from the park. I've spent many days here and hanging out in her office while I wait for her to get off from work, especially in the summer. The weirdest part is that she doesn't work in the bank part but in the business part on the top floor. She complains a lot about overtime and having to finish some of her projects on weekends, but at least she has the best view of the town from her window.

"Okay. I'll be here. At the park." For two whole hours, now that I think about it. What am I gonna talk to Lily about for two whole hours?! This is already a disaster.

"You better be!" Mom laughs. I try to smile back, but I feel sick. She notices right away, her smile turning into a deep frown in seconds. "Are you okay?"

Darn you, Laser Eyes! I take a deep breath to steady myself. I have to do this. The only thing worse than having a bad date is not having a date at all. And I really do want to see Bri. Talking on the phone is fun, but it's not the same as seeing her in person. I miss her.

"I'm okay, I promise." I open my door before I lose my nerve. "Bye! Love you!"

Mom doesn't say anything as I hop out of the car, but when I turn around to shut it behind me, she gives me a small smile. "Love you too. Call me if you feel sick, and I'll pick you up early."

Gratitude surges up in my chest and gives me courage. Mom doesn't know what I'm about to do, but she wants me to know I can call her if it doesn't go well. It's like accidental encouragement. I nod, determined, and close the door. I wave as she drives away, and then I turn and face the park. All alone.

Oh man. Here we go.

I go to our normal meet-up place: Pavilion B, perfectly placed between the dog park and the swings. Bri lounges on a long, wooden seat next to a picnic table, wearing a flannel jacket and sneakers. Despite being nervous about my (sort-of) date, pure joy fills me from my head to my toes. Seeing her in person is just like it used to be, before private school and loneliness got in the way.

"Bri!" I run as fast as I can to Pavilion B. She jumps up at the sound of my voice, already grinning, and then we're hugging and screaming. I don't even care who's looking because I'm so happy!

We take a breath and Bri holds me at arm's length. Her dark brown eyes are alight with happiness, but they're kind of intense too.

"What're you doing?" I ask, still grinning.

Bri grins back. "Memorizing your face so I know what you look like after your mom kills you."

I snort out a laugh and Bri squishes my cheeks with her palms. "Stop, stop!"

"I won't! I can't even believe you, Nova. You have secret friends *and* a secret viral Instagram *and* a secret girlfriend?! Who are you! I leave you alone for a few months and you go rogue."

"Lily isn't my girlfriend," I correct her. I'll just . . . ignore the rest.

"Not with that attitude!" Bri winks and finally stops squishing my cheeks. Her grin is replaced with fierce determination. "Which reminds me—we've gotta make sure this date goes perfectly."

I don't like that *we* are on a sort-of date with Lily, but honestly, I can use the help. I don't want to mess this up. I think I'd die of embarrassment. I mimic Bri's serious expression. "Let's make a plan."

"Okay. First, we need something to do." Bri puts her hands on her hips and looks around. There are kids on the swings and the dog park is empty . . . not a great sign. I feel sweaty again. Ugh.

"Maybe we can just talk?" I suggest.

"Sure, but it's better if we can *do* something while we talk. Ugh, I should have brought Carl!"

"No way. He'd bite Lily and she'd never talk to me again."

"Trauma bonding!" Bri says, and I giggle. She starts to say something else, but her eyes widen, and she gasps. "Nova, don't panic."

"I'm panicking," I say immediately. I'm not, though, not yet. She probably just saw a big dog. "What's the matter?"

"She's here." Bri's voice is hushed.

Oh no. I don't think she's talking about a dog.

I turn around, because even if I'm a sweaty, panicked mess, I do want to see her. And when I do, I'm stunned into silence. Lily looks so cute! She's wearing a black jacket over a cute flowered dress with black leggings underneath, and wow is that makeup?! Mom would murder me if I even tried to wear eye shadow. Lily smiles at me, and I swear I'm staring directly into the sun.

"Hi, Nova," Lily says. She seems almost shy? But there's no way. Why would she be shy around me? She glances at Bri next and smiles too. "Gabriella, right?"

"Just Bri," Bri says. She grins and bumps my shoulder, shocking me out of my admiration stupor. "I'm this one's best friend! She's stunned right now, but she'll recover soon, don't worry."

"Bri!" I hiss, but Lily laughs.

"It's okay. I'm really glad we can hang out." Lily sits down and I automatically do too, even though Bri just said we should do something. Bri sighs but hurries around the table to sit across from me and Lily.

"What do y'all usually do at this park?" Lily asks. She swings her legs back and forth under the picnic table, like maybe she's nervous. She can't be nervous; I'm nervous! A million options cycle through my mind. Bri and I normally just talk, and sometimes sit on the swings, and sometimes beg dog owners to pet their dogs. But suddenly all that sounds painfully boring. I could say that we normally plan elaborate heists. Or discuss paintings? Wait, that also sounds boring!

Bri kicks my shin under the table. She looks amused. "Your friend's talking to you, Nova."

Ugh, I can't stand Bri sometimes. She knows I'm trying to figure out a cool answer! I look at Lily, who's waiting patiently, and I blurt out the first thing that comes to mind. "We write plays and perform them."

Lily's eyes grow round. "Really?"

I start to really lean into my lie, but Bri kicks me again. Harder this time. I shoot her a glare and she glares back. Ugh. UGH.

"No," I admit sheepishly. "I just thought that sounded cool."

Lily looks confused and Bri laughs. "Listen, Lily. Nova's a pathological liar."

"I am not!" My face heats up with shame. She can't tell Lily everything about me! She'll hate me!

"Look, she's lying already." Bri laughs to herself. "Tip for being Nova's friend—always ask her things twice. The first answer is usually a lie, but you can guilt her into the truth the second time."

This is horrible. Humiliating! But Lily doesn't seem mad. She just seems curious.

"Why lie?" Lily asks. And she's so sincere, so nonjudgmental, I end up telling the truth.

"I don't want you to think I'm lame."

"You're not lame!" Lily smiles at me and my heart flutters pitifully against my ribs. "I think you're cool. You don't have to lie to me for me to think that."

"Oh." I don't know what to say. I feel like a small, anxious knot in my chest loosens, unraveling terror and apprehension. Maybe . . . maybe I can't disappoint Lily. Maybe she likes me for who I am.

Bri pounces on my stunned silence. She's barely holding back laughter, like this is the best day of her life. "Glad we got that settled! Now, Nova, tell Lily what we actually do on Saturdays."

I turn to Lily, shyly, and ask, "How do you feel about petting dogs?"

Lily grins, looking right into my eyes like Bri's not even here. Like I'm the only girl in the whole world. "I love dogs."

I swear I'm gonna float away. I feel so happy I could fly into the air like a balloon and never come down.

"One problem." Bri's voice brings me back to earth. "Looks like there are no dogs today."

"Bummer," Lily says. She kicks her feet again, and the nervous look is back. "If it's not too much trouble, I have a suggestion?"

I glance at Bri and she nods. I turn to Lily. "What do you have in mind?"

CHAPTER 13

Sometimes when I read teen books about high school and crushes (Mom doesn't know, but she doesn't mind as long as I'm reading), the main characters will say how "hot" their crush is. Even if they're just standing around and looking broody, the main characters are all so happy and squealing in their heads that their crush is so "hot." I never really got that, or what that means.

But now, watching Lily with her cute baseball helmet on, bat in her hands, concentrating fiercely on the pitching machine in front of her, I totally get it.

"Are you gonna survive this?" Bri teases under her breath.

"Do not talk to me right now."

Bri snorts out a laugh, but I literally can't focus on her. I'm enraptured by Lily, how she swings her bat at the fuzzy yellow ball with deadly precision, how the resulting crack that sounds like thunder and lightning is crackling in my brain. When she suggested batting cages, the nice, warm indoor ones, I wasn't sure because I'm definitely not athletic. But now I'm wondering how I can convince Lily to come here every day.

Lily swings and misses her first ball in ten tries. She turns to us, scratching her arm in embarrassment. "Aww man, sorry y'all had to see that!"

I squeak out reassurances, but as soon as she goes back to swinging, I turn to Bri.

"Will you help me plan my proposal?"

Bri nearly passes out trying to hold in a laugh, and I'm finally able to smile through my dumbstruck staring. There's just so much information to process! I didn't know Lily played baseball (softball?). I know she mentioned practice before, but I was too shy to ask what it was for. And now I'm remembering when we shook hands, her hand wasn't soft like I thought it would be. That makes sense! For some reason, I don't feel shy anymore. I want to know everything about Lily, everything she'll tell me.

Oh man. I think my crush just leveled up.

Lily comes to the fence, smiling. She's just a little sweaty, but man, that makes me like her more! I'm sweaty and I've just been standing here.

"Do you want to try?" Lily asks us, but she's looking at me.

"Not me," Bri says. She holds up her hands, grinning. "These are for piano, not sports."

Bri literally hates playing piano; she's turning her down for me. I could cry from gratitude.

"I've never played before," I hedge, but Lily's smile just gets wider.

"I can show you," she says, and I'm back to floating away.

I'm not proud to say this, but for the next thirty minutes, I completely forget Bri exists. All I can think about is Lily showing me how to hold a bat, how her hands gently correct my grip and I drop the bat anyway because I'm a swamp creature that doesn't deserve to be so close to a girl this cool and beautiful and talented. She throws a ball for me to hit, and I miss—wish I was joking—seven times in a row because I keep looking at Lily's face and not the ball. But then on the eighth try, I hit it! I scream so loud I scare myself, and Lily gives me a huge hug. I'm pretty sure I passed away and now I'm a ghost.

After that, our batting cage time is over, so we put our coats on and join Bri—oh yeah, my best friend who's been watching me act like a lovesick idiot. We make the trek back to our favorite pavilion. Bri smirks at me and I know I'll never live this down.

"You both did so good!" Bri says. She nudges me with her elbow. "Even the strikeout queen here."

"Nova did great." I'm surprised to hear some fierce defensiveness in Lily's tone. She looks at me, her cheeks still pink from the exercise (right?). "The first time Dad took me here, I struck out so much, I cried. So that's way better than me."

"How long have you played?" I ask.

"Since I was four."

"How did I not know this?!" Oops—I didn't mean to say that out loud! But Lily just laughs.

"We've never talked before!"

"Speaking of . . ." Bri sits down at our normal pavilion, rubbing her hands together against the cold. "Why did you decide to talk to Nova now? Just curious."

I tense, but Lily doesn't look bothered. She sits down next to me, closer than she was before. "Honestly, I was too shy." Lily looks at me and I'm dazzled by her smile again. "I've wanted to be your friend since we worked on that science project together."

"Last year?" I can't hide the surprise in my voice. I remember that project because Lily and Isaac Davidson were in my group, and Isaac did absolutely *nothing*. But Lily and I worked super hard, and all three of us got a 97. But that was last year, in sixth grade. She's wanted to be my friend for that long?

"Yeah." Lily laughs, a little awkwardly. "That's why I felt so bad when you thought I just wanted to hang out with Kevin. No offense to him, but you're cooler."

"Not according to twenty thousand people," Bri says, but she's smiling at me. She looks delighted and relieved, and I know we're thinking the same thing—we can trust Lily. I don't know about Kylie and Raina, not yet, but I don't think I have anything to worry about with Lily.

"How do you like Instagram, Nova?" Lily asks me. "I hardly ever use mine. I'm always on TikTok."

"We're not supposed to have social media anyway," I say, guilt in my voice.

"Excuse you! I'm thirteen!" Lily sits up straighter and kind of puffs out her chest, and Bri and I laugh.

"I'm not," Bri says. She blows out an anxious breath and fidgets. "Our moms'll kill us if they find out."

"I kind of wish mine would find out." I wince. I didn't mean to say that. I don't want them to think I can't handle it.

Lily and Bri frown at me. "You don't like it?" Lily asks.

My first urge is to lie. But Bri and Lily are waiting, watching me patiently. And something tells me they won't be disappointed. I take a shaky breath. "It's just . . . it's really hard to keep up with. I have to take so many pictures, and then I have to edit them, and Kevin hates the camera and always tries to run away from me. It takes so long that it cuts into my study time."

"Only you would be sad about that," Bri teases, but Lily looks deeply serious.

"That does sound like a lot. Can we help?"

I smile at them both as Bri nods too. "No, but thanks. I like seeing the comments. Well, except the mean ones."

"You get mean comments?!" Now Bri looks outraged. "How could they? Kevin is adorable!"

"Just tag me next time," Lily says. Her tone is just as serious as her expression. "I don't mind fighting weird adults."

I laugh and Bri does too, and I really wish I could stay here forever.

But I can't, because only ten minutes later, I hear Mom honk her horn. I glance at my phone and groan—she's fifteen minutes early! Mom, please!

"Is that your mom?" Lily asks. I nod and she waves. Mom doesn't wave back. Uh-oh.

"Gotta go." I hop off the bench and Bri stands up. We hug and Bri squishes my cheeks.

"I'll see you in two weeks! Seriously, let me know if I can help with your Instagram, okay?" She gives me an exaggerated wink. "And anything else."

I roll my eyes, grinning. "Bye, Bri." I turn to Lily, shy again. "Umm, thanks for hanging out with us."

"You bet." Lily matches my grin. "See you at school?"

I nod, joy swelling pleasantly in my chest. "Okay. See you Monday."

I wave to Bri and Lily, and jog to Mom's car. I get in the front seat, vibrating with happiness. I don't even mind when Mom's Laser Eyes notice.

"Who was that with Bri?" Mom asks as we pull away from the park. "A new friend?"

I look out the window and watch Lily and Bri wave and separate, Bri to her mom's car, Lily to a red truck. I smile at Lily until I can't see her anymore.

"Yeah. Maybe a really good friend."

CHAPTER 14

"Will Kevin pose with us today?" Kylie bounces on her toes, like she can't contain her excitement from spilling out of her body.

"Uhh . . ." I search for him and finally find him pressed unhappily under the couch. His ears are flat against his head and his tail lashes the floor back and forth. "I don't think he's in the posing mood."

"Aww, man." Raina looks like she might cry.

"He'll probably come out eventually," Lily offers. She's standing really close to me, so close the hairs on our arms are touching. My heart is doing its running-a-marathon thing, but it doesn't feel so panicky now. It's getting familiar, and kind of . . . good? Fun? I don't know how to describe it, but I'm happy she's here. And that she likes me enough to stand next to me.

After our almost-date at the park, Lily and I have been hanging out a lot more. She waits for me to get to school, and we talk about homework and softball teams and how country music is the death to the music industry (Lily said Carrie Underwood isn't so bad, and I threatened to end our friendship. She just laughed). We talk about how my mom is strict, and Lily sometimes wishes her parents were stricter, because they're gone a lot and they let her do whatever. We talk about vegetarians, and how cats are great but not as good as dogs (that's definitely Lily's extremely incorrect opinion), and how it would be cool to be an astronaut, but also maybe a zookeeper or anything that doesn't involve math. Bri says it sounds an awful lot like we might be almost-dating for real. I told her to stop being delusional, but secretly, I wish she was right.

Though everything has been great with Lily this past week,

nothing else is working out. I told Bri and Lily Instagram wasn't so bad, but it really is. I spend almost two hours a day just editing pictures and deleting DMs, and then I still have to study! We started an even harder unit in math, and I've been studying nonstop—so much that I'm kind of neglecting my other classes. It sucks so much; last night I fell asleep at my desk and woke up with a really bad pain in my neck. And now Kylie and Raina are here because they asked to come over, and even though I'm not sure if I trust them, I couldn't say no when Lily looked at me. I feel like I'm falling apart, but I'm determined to keep going. The Harris girls get things done: If Mom can work three jobs for me, I can do all this for her. And Bri. And Lily. I just have to find a way to make it all work.

"What should we do until he comes out?" Kylie asks, bringing me back to the present. She glances at the living room TV but shakes her head right after. "I don't want to watch something. I want to do something!"

"We could do our homework?" I regret it as soon as I say it.

Cool people don't want to do their homework! But I do . . . I'm really far behind in math now. And I haven't read any of my chapters for English.

"We can do that later," Kylie says, and my stomach drops. I really need to, but she's right . . .

"Maybe we can start." Lily surprises me by disagreeing with Kylie. She gives me a small smile and the back of her hand brushes mine, sending tingles all the way up my arm. "I have a lot of homework to do."

Kylie grumbles, but Raina shrugs and grabs her backpack. I start to take my stuff to the kitchen table, but Kylie plops down in the middle of the living room floor. Okay . . . guess we're studying in here! I sit next to her and Lily sits next to me, and soon we're all arguing about the discussion questions for *Where the Red Fern Grows.*

"I don't know why we have to read all these sad dog books," Kylie complains. "This is, like, the third one."

"I get the message of *Old Yeller,*" Lily says, "because he was a hero at the end. And I guess the moral is that we should get our dogs their rabies shots. But what was the point of killing the dogs in this one?"

"Wait, the dogs die?" My stomach clenches in shock. "Both of them?!"

"You haven't read it yet?" Lily seems surprised.

I shake my head, despair in my heart. Because of Instagram and these secret hang outs, I haven't had the time. I'm suddenly very aware of how far behind I am in my classes. "No, I was gonna read it tonight! How'd they die?"

"Dan got eaten by a mountain lion," Raina grunts.

"No way—"

"And Ann died of sadness," Kylie adds. "What a drag, huh?"

A drag?! That's the saddest thing I've ever heard. Oh my God.

"Are you crying?" Kylie asks, a mischievous grin on her face.

"No." I'm lying. I'm on the verge of tears. I can't believe they both died! Mrs. Paulson can't keep getting away with this.

"Don't act like you didn't cry," Lily teases Kylie. "You called me and everything."

"Ugh, don't tell everyone my business!" Kylie is trying to

look stern, but she's laughing. I smile too, despite the sad plot points. I wipe my eyes and Kevin wanders into my lap, meowing softly. He purrs as I pet his head and bumps the top of his head against my chin.

"Well, at least I didn't have to read it," I say, slowly stroking Kevin. Everyone is quiet, just staring at me. I pause, suddenly nervous. "What?"

"Kevin," Kylie hisses. Her eyes are round and bright with excitement. "He came out!"

Oh yeah! I look down at him in surprise. He purrs again and paws at my cheek.

"He must have sensed you were sad," Raina says, her voice hushed in awe.

I look up just as Kylie snaps a picture of me with her phone. I blink and she grins. "You can put this on your Instagram!"

My phone lights up with a text. I open it and I see myself, surprise on my face and my eyes wet with tears. Kevin is really cute, his massive form taking up the whole picture. His eyes are closed as he rubs his ears against my chin.

"This is pretty good," I admit. I'm sort of relieved. It's hard to take good pictures all the time and Kylie is a natural. Tonight's content is sorted!

"Can I pet him while he's distracted?" Raina asks.

I nod, and she timidly approaches. Kevin looks at her, but I'm scratching his favorite spot behind his head so he doesn't seem to mind. Raina reaches out slowly and pets him, grinning, and Kylie takes her picture too. Everyone ends up crowding beside me as Kylie takes all of our pictures. I smile into the camera, and this almost feels like what real friends do.

"This one is so cute!" Kylie squeals. She shows us the picture. It's all of us grinning into the camera while Kevin looks slightly annoyed that the attention isn't on him. It is pretty good! I'm already planning on spacing out the content, so I can take some time away from Instagram and actually read the books assigned instead of hearing spoilers from Kylie.

"I don't know . . ." Raina seems anxious for the first time since I've known her. Which isn't that long, but still.

"Do you not like it?" I ask. I study Raina's face on the

picture. She's smiling and happy, and Kevin's tail is curled around her wrist. She looks normal to me! I think we all look pretty good.

"It's the angle," Raina says. She looks worried. "My face is down too much, so it looks like I have a double chin."

Lily stiffens beside me. She looks at Raina, and her eyes are sharp and dark. Her smile is long gone. "What're you trying to say?"

Uh-oh. Lily's voice is full of danger, but it's like Raina doesn't even feel it. She just blinks at Lily and says, "Nothing, I just don't want Nova to post a picture where I look fat to all her followers."

Yikes. Oh yikes, this is really bad. Kylie looks at me, her eyes wide with panic, but I don't know what to do. I can practically feel the rage rising off Lily like steam off a bowl of soup.

"What's so wrong with being fat, Raina?" Lily's voice is practically a whisper, but *I* am afraid, and it's not even directed at me. Kevin kneads his claws nervously into my leg, his ears pricked and alert.

Raina looks uncomfortable. "I don't know, it's just—"

"It's just what?" Lily's voice is deadly calm. "It's just that you don't want to look like me?"

Raina finally seems to get it. Understanding dawns on her face, and she immediately seems upset. "No, Lily, I didn't mean it like that."

"It doesn't matter how you meant it. It's what you said."

The tension is thick in the living room. Kylie and I look at each other in silent horror. Oh God, what do I say? What do I do?

Kevin jumps off my lap. He meows loudly, making all of us flinch. He rubs his head against Lily's hand, then trots to Raina and purrs against her side. Everyone cautiously relaxes. I breathe a sigh of relief—the tension is gone. At least for now. I think for a minute before I break the silence.

"I won't post it," I say. I look at Raina, then Lily. "But I think we all look great, so I might put it as my phone background!"

Lily's murderous expression softens. "It's okay. Maybe I'll put it on mine too."

"Me too!" Kylie hastily agrees.

Raina hesitates but nods. "Me too. It is a good picture."

Okay! Whew. Crisis averted. Kevin trots between all of us as we finish the discussion questions and our science worksheets. Everything is normal again, almost, but when I glance over at Lily, she seems kind of sad. And Raina doesn't say much for an entire hour.

I just got into this friend group, maybe, but I can already tell it's in trouble. I don't think this is the end of this argument at all.

CHAPTER 15

When Kylie's mom arrives to pick them up, Lily hesitates at the door. She looks at me, a complicated expression on her face. "Can I stay a little longer, Nova? Just us?"

Oh. *Oh!* I definitely want to hang out, just us! But the time—I check frantically, but it's just 4:10. We still have fifty minutes before Mom is supposed to get home. And things were really tense with Raina earlier. I bet she wants to talk about it.

"Yeah," I say. "Of course!"

Lily gives me a relieved smile. She sends a quick text on her phone and then jogs outside to talk to Kylie's mom, and I wave at Kylie and Raina from the porch. They wave back as Lily returns.

"My dad said he'll pick me up at four forty-five. Is that okay?"

She remembered about Mom! I smile. "Yeah, that's okay." I open my front door, and Lily goes into the house again.

But once we're alone, I'm full of nervous silence. Does she want to talk? Or do more homework? Or something else?! Lily also looks nervous. She shuffles her feet a little, not looking at me.

Kevin yowls at me from upstairs, jolting me from my nervousness. I point at the ceiling, which seems really dumb now that I'm doing it. "Do you want to go to my room?"

Lily seems excited. "Yes, I'd love to!"

Okay. I won't make this weird at all. I climb the steps, but I'm aware that Lily is behind me, and also that I've never thought about climbing stairs before. Have my legs always moved this way? Am I doing it wrong?

Kevin meets me at the door. He purrs and rubs against my legs but stiffens when he sees Lily behind me.

"Be nice," I tell him. Kevin huffs and trots back into my room.

"I don't think he likes me," Lily says. But she doesn't sound sad. She sounds amused, like she's about to laugh at a joke.

"He does! He just hates that he doesn't get all the attention when you're here." I lead the way into my room, but I don't know what to do when I get inside. "Umm, here it is!"

Lily wanders around, fascination on her face. "I love your posters! What band is that?"

"The Gazette." Oh man, my room is a minefield. How do I explain I like metal music that's not even in English? But I reach for the courage I had at the park. Lily didn't laugh at me about being a vegetarian. Or for being lame and doing kid stuff with Bri. I take a deep breath. "They're a rock/metal band. I really like the instruments and, umm, everything." Oh God, that was horrible.

But Lily doesn't laugh. She asks me more questions about them, and we even listen to some of my favorite songs on my phone. Then, Lily introduces me to Korean R&B, which I didn't know even existed?! We listen to a few of her favorite songs, and she texts me a bunch of other ones to listen to later, which I will *definitely* do.

I glance at the time: 4:26. She has to go in twenty minutes and we didn't even talk! At least, not about the important things. I sneak a look at Lily. She's sitting on my bed, Kevin purring in her lap, scrolling happily through my playlist on my phone. She doesn't seem sad anymore, but I should probably ask about that argument. Every day gets more and more tense at the lunch table between Lily and Raina.

"Umm, Lily?"

"Hmm?" Lily looks up from my phone.

I take a nervous breath. "Umm . . . about earlier . . ."

Lily's happiness dries up in an instant. The stormy expression is back. Anxiety churns in my gut. Maybe I shouldn't have said anything. "What about it?"

Lily's voice is guarded, but she's not super mad like earlier. I try to pick my words carefully. "I'm sorry about what Raina said. That wasn't cool."

Lily seems surprised. Some of the storm calms and it's more like a light rain, maybe. "You don't think I was overreacting? I feel kind of bad."

"She hurt your feelings, right?" When Lily nods reluctantly, I continue. "Then no, not an overreaction. But honestly, I don't get what she's saying. She looked great in that picture. We all did! Plus, Kevin is the star anyway."

Lily smiles a little. She pets Kevin's head a few times before speaking. "I try not to let it bother me. Like, I know I'm fat. I have eyes. But when Raina says it, she makes it sound like a bad thing." Lily rubs the back of her neck, sighing. She's looking firmly at Kevin and not me. "I don't know. We've been friends for forever—I just can't believe she'd say stuff like that. I know it's her mom getting into her head, but it sucks. Sometimes I get so mad at her I just want to punch something. And then right after, I get really sad."

"It's puberty," I say, hoping to be helpful. "Mrs. Helen said mood swings are really common."

Lily finally looks at me. Her eyes are wet with tears, which makes my heart hurt so much I feel like it's going to burst. But she's also smiling, and though her eyes are full of tears, they're really soft and looking at me with gratitude.

"Nova . . . thanks. I'm sorry I made everything weird downstairs."

"Don't be sorry." I pause, thinking. I know, logically, that Lily is a few sizes bigger than me. But I don't see that as a bad thing. I like Lily for how smart and kind and cool she is, and she's so pretty! Her eyes are big and warm, and her eyelashes are super long, and her nose gets cute little wrinkles on it when she's concentrating on a math problem. I hate that Raina can't see any of that and just made her feel bad. I pick my words carefully. "I'm sorry that Raina is being a jerk, but I don't think you have anything to be sad about. I won't call you fat if you don't want, but I really don't think it's a bad thing. It's just a part of you, and I like all of you, if that makes sense."

Lily's eyes widen, and mine do too as I realize what I said. I said I like her! Oh no, I wasn't supposed to say that! I'm staring into Lily's pretty brown eyes, and it's like neither of us can look away.

"I like all of you too," Lily says. Her voice is quiet, hushed, and she's so close her breath tickles my nose.

"Even that I'm a weird vegetarian?"

A smile tugs on Lily's lips. "Especially that you're a weird, smart, beautiful, funny vegetarian."

Smart. Beautiful. And weird. But coming from Lily, that feels like the sweetest thing I've ever heard.

Lily puts one hand on my knee. My heart is going so fast, I'm sure I'll pass out. But I wouldn't dare move because then I wouldn't get to feel her warm hand on my skin.

"Nova, I'm gonna ask you something."

"Okay," I squeak.

Lily searches my eyes, hers wide and anxious. She looks scared, but I guarantee she's not a fraction as scared as I am. "When you said you liked all of me, do you mean as a friend? Or . . ."

It's so hard to breathe. I don't want to ruin this. I like Lily so, so much, and her friendship means a lot to me. I don't want to ruin what I've worked so hard to build. But I promised I wouldn't lie to her. A promise that's been easier and easier to keep, and even if this secret is something I'm aching to hold close, even though my brain immediately starts thinking of options to play off what I said as a joke and stay friends, I push through and keep my promise.

"No," I say, my heart threatening to jump out of my chest and into my mouth, "not in a friend way."

Lily does a little gasp that sets my anxiety into overdrive. Is that a good gasp or a bad one?! Or a neutral one, since we just said that words and descriptions can be neutral—

"I don't mean in a friend way either."

I blink at Lily, barely comprehending what she just said. "You . . . you don't?"

"No, I don't." A slow smile spreads on her face. "I mean that I like you, a lot. And I have for months!"

It's my turn to gasp. Before I can stop myself, I say, "You have the weird puberty too?!" I cover my mouth with both hands. Oh God why did I say that—

But Lily laughs. Really hard. So hard she's shaking and tears come to her eyes. "Yes, I have the *unusual* puberty too. I think it's just called being a lesbian, though."

"I don't know about labels yet," I admit, "but I know that I like you. A lot. For months, umm, too."

Lily grins and she gently takes my face in her hands. Her palms are warm and my skin tingles pleasantly against her touch. She looks right into my eyes, grin euphoric, and says, "I'm going to kiss you."

I almost pass out on the spot. I don't know if I'm ready! But at the same time, I know I am. My heart is thudding frantically against my ribs, and I know my hands are sweaty, but my whole body is singing yes, yes, *yes*. So I gather all my courage, nod, and say, "Please do."

And she does. Lily leans in and presses her lips to mine. And she's soft and tastes vaguely of the snacks we had earlier, and I get a burning sensation all over my body. I'm on fire and I want nothing more than to burn.

My first thought is that I'm probably the happiest I've ever been in my life.

My second thought is that Mom is going to kill me.

But I dismiss that second thought when Lily pulls away, and we're just grinning at each other like we're the only two people in the whole world.

"Wow." I don't know what else to say. What else can you say when your dream comes true?

"Yeah." Lily giggles suddenly and I do too. I want to kiss her again, but am I allowed? Is this a one-time thing, or are we—

We both jump when a car horn sounds outside. I check the time on my phone: 4:50! We're late!

"That's Dad!" Lily hops off my bed and hastily shoves everything in her backpack. I hover nervously, and she shoulders her bag and looks at me. She smiles.

"I'll see you tomorrow?"

"Yeah," I say. "For sure. And umm . . ."

"Are we girlfriends?" Lily blurts out. She covers her mouth like she didn't mean to say that.

I laugh because I feel the same. "I was going to ask you! I mean I would like that, if you do?"

"I do," Lily says. Her face is like the sun. "I really do."

"Okay," I say, almost more to myself. "We're girlfriends." Together. In a relationship. Oh my God, I never thought it would happen to me! I still can't believe it.

Lily's dad leans on the horn, and she mutters a rare curse under her breath. "Okay, I gotta go. See you tomorrow, Nova!"

I wave as Lily hurries out of my home, starstruck. "Bye," I say, but I'm sure she can't hear me. I watch from my window as she runs outside and hops into an old red truck. Her dad pulls away, and it's only when she's gone that it hits me: Lily Weston likes me. Lily is my *girlfriend*! I whoop and jump into the air, startling Kevin. I pick him up and spin him around, ignoring his groans.

"Lily's my girlfriend!" I yell to the ceiling. Kevin grumbles in my arms. I'm so happy I could die! But then I hear another, familiar car, and I drop Kevin in shock. Mom. She's here already. Five minutes early! If Lily's dad hadn't gotten here when he did, we would have been caught.

I stare at her car, and for a second, I'm hit with terrible disappointment. I'm so incredibly happy right now, and I can't even tell her why. I wish I could tell Mom everything. I wish she could accept all of my labels and not just some of them. She likes *smart* and *good daughter*. But she would never accept *vegetarian* or *bad at math*. And probably never, ever *Lily's girlfriend*. I watch her unlock the door from my window, and despite feeling that incredible happiness a second ago, I really want to cry.

I hear Mom open the front door and call for me. I take a deep breath, stuff down all my joy and sadness so she can't see, and go downstairs to meet her.

CHAPTER 16

I have a terrible headache, and it's not from lack of sleep.

I'm not saying that's not a part of it though. It's been a week since the magical afternoon Lily kissed me, but my bliss didn't last forever. I still have so much to do, and I'm just barely caught up with school. Instagram takes so, so much time to manage, but I don't want to let it go because everyone loves Kevin. And I have a math test coming up, so I've started sleeping less in favor of studying more. I wake up groggy and irritated every day.

But now I'm looking at my Instagram and my head hurts worse, because I'm on Tiffany's profile. And the latest picture is her holding a baby blue bento box, showing the camera her rice that's shaped like an Easter egg. And Bri is next to her, grinning, posing with an identical box.

I grip my phone as tight as I grit my teeth. What's so special about those fancy lunch boxes?! And why does Bri look so much happier with Tiffany? Why can she be tagged in Tiffany's pictures, but not mine? Now I'm sad, plus the headache. Must be the mood swings I told Lily about. Puberty is evil.

Lily sits next to me, and I look up at her to smile. It's just us at my house today; Kylie has cheer tryouts and Raina is hanging out with her grandma. Not that I'm complaining! It's only been a week, but I'm so happy. Having her here beside me dulls the sting from the infamous Tiffany.

"Instagram got you down again?" Lily asks. She snuggles right up to my side, like she's not shy around me at all anymore. I still get shy and overwhelmed that she even likes me, but I'm glad Lily is comfortable. Especially around *me*.

"Sort of . . ."

Lily frowns at my phone. "Who's that with Bri?"

A huge sigh escapes before I can stop it. Lily raises her eyebrows, inviting me to go on. I would have hidden how I felt a few weeks ago, but now I trust Lily. Almost as much as I do Bri, and this is the one thing I can't talk to Bri about.

"Her name's Tiffany. She's my nemesis, even though we've never met." I stare at her smiling face and more sadness tugs at my gut. "She might be Bri's new best friend."

"Oh." Lily's voice is heavy with sympathy.

"Yeah." I sigh again, and this time my eyes sting with tears. "I don't want Bri to forget about me. But it's my fault we didn't get to go to private school together, so I feel like I can't say anything about Tiffany and her stupid lunches."

"What do you mean it's your fault?" I hesitate, but Lily puts her hand over mine. I look up and she's watching me with that intense expression, like she can see into my brain. But there's a soft edge to it, unlike Mom's and Mr. Wickett's Laser Eyes. "You can tell me."

And I do. I tell her all about how I wasn't smart enough for private school and how sad and disappointed Mom was. I tell her about how jealous I am of Bri's new friends, so much I can't even talk with her about them. I tell her my plan and how I stay up late every night studying so I can retest in just a few more weeks so I can right my wrong. Lily listens, never looking away from me once. When I'm done, she nods slowly.

"Well, first, thank you for telling me. Honestly, that's a lot to hold in."

"Yeah." I blink away tears and Lily holds my hand, squeezing it gently in her rough palms.

"I think you should tell Bri how you feel. Don't make that face! I know it's scary, but you really are best friends. I could see it when we hung out."

I shake my head. "I don't want her to know I'm jealous. I . . . I won't be . . ."

"Perfect?" Lily suggests.

I hesitate, turning that over in my head. It's an uncomfortable admission, one that doesn't have the best connotation (another vocab word!), but it feels true. As much as I don't like it. "Yeah, I think so. I don't want to be a bad friend."

"It's not bad to be jealous. But maybe it is to not be honest."

I don't say anything, thinking, and Lily keeps talking.

"Anyway, I'm proud of you for studying and being so smart. But . . ." Lily smiles at me. "Personally, I'm glad you didn't get into that private school. Even if Tiffany looks like a drag."

I smile back, and some of the tightness in my chest loosens. Lily's right, isn't she? I failed, and it sucked, but if I hadn't, I wouldn't be here with Lily. And that's not so bad, right? And Lily agrees with me about Tiffany, so I'm feeling a hundred times better.

I put my phone down and hug Lily as tight as I can. She laughs and hugs me back.

"Does that mean I'm right?" Lily teases.

"Maybe." But when I pull away, I'm grinning. "Thanks, Lily. I'm kind of glad I didn't get into private school too. Though then I wouldn't have to do Mr. Wickett's math."

"Ugh, tell me about it," Lily groans. "I wish I'd gotten in too!"

We laugh and study and cuddle while we talk about school until Lily's dad picks her up at four forty-five. But when I'm alone, I think really hard about what Lily said. I've been fighting so hard for private school, but . . . do I even want to go? I don't want to leave Lily behind. I don't want to leave Kylie and Raina either. I was really lonely, but now I'm not. So . . . does that mean . . .

I don't have to study for the private school exam anymore?

My stomach feels queasy at the thought. I've been working so hard. And Bri might forget me. I don't want to have to choose between Bri and Lily . . .

But maybe I don't have to. Maybe I can talk to Bri, like Lily said.

When Mom gets home, she kisses the top of my head. "You look upset," she says, laying her keys down on the coffee table. "You okay?"

I want to lie, but this time I tell the truth, because my mind is made up. "Soon I will be."

I'm lying down in my bed when my phone starts singing. Kevin growls irritably, rolling over on his back while I reach for my phone. I laugh but wince when the screen's bright light sends pain needling through my head. I've had a headache for two days straight, and I thought lying down in the dark might help. But talking to Bri might help too.

I accept the FaceTime call and Bri's kitchen pops into view. I don't see her though.

"Hello?"

"Nova!" Bri's face appears, like she's leaning from the side. "Mom's finally letting me bake by myself!"

"Oh, cool!" Bri loves to cook, but her mom is always careful about supervising. "What're you making?"

"Cookies. I'll bring you some Saturday."

I smile at her. "Hopefully they're not oatmeal raisin."

"What kind of psychopath do you think I am?" Bri snorts. She leans closer to the camera. "Why is it so dark in your room? Were you sleeping?"

"No." I sigh. "My head hurts, so I'm taking a break."

"Are you sick?" Bri disappears from view again and I hear clanking sounds from off-screen. "Tiffany got a cold from making out with Aaron. Which is, like, kill me. Did I tell you that Aaron started sitting with us at lunch? They can't keep their hands off each other, and me and Skylar are just sitting there awkwardly. It's so weird and rude! Thank God you and Lily aren't like that."

I don't say anything at first. Tiffany continues to be the worst, so I feel savagely vindicated (two vocab words!). But also . . . I don't know Tiffany. I haven't even tried to get to know her. She might be great, except for making out with her boyfriend instead of eating lunch, which I agree is weird and kind of gross.

"Nova?" Bri's head pops back into frame. She's frowning anxiously. "You okay? Do you think you have a fever? Not that your mom would let you stay home."

"Bri . . ." I take a deep breath and hug Kevin for strength. He purrs softly, and the vibrations calm me. "I'm sorry."

Bri's frown deepens and she abandons whatever she was making. I can see her whole face now. "For what?"

"I've been kind of jealous of Tiffany. And Skylar, but mostly

Tiffany. I . . . I feel like since I'm not with you at your new school, you'll forget about me."

Bri's eyebrows pinch together. "No way, Nova! I'm not gonna forget you. We hang out every two weeks."

"I know, but . . . you never post pictures of us on your Instagram. But you do with Tiffany. So . . ."

"Oh no." Bri looks stricken. "I'm sorry, Nova! I only did that because if Mami finds out I have it, she will kill me. And if she sees you on there, she'll kill you too and then tell your mom. And you'll get double killed."

"Oh." She was protecting me? "So Tiffany's mom doesn't care?"

"Nope. That's why I don't post Skylar either. His dad would be so mad."

I stay silent, a little stunned. Lily was right. I was honest and Bri wasn't mad at all.

"Are you okay?" Bri asks. She twists the collar of her shirt anxiously. "How long were you upset about this? You should have talked to me!"

"I know. I'm sorry. I just . . . I've been messing up so much lately, I didn't want you to know I couldn't even do long-distance friendship right either."

"It's not that long-distance," Bri says, smiling. "Listen, I'm gonna ask Mami if you can come over some Saturdays. Or I can come to your house."

"Really?"

"Yeah! You're my best friend, not Tiffany. No offense, Tiffany."

I smile at my phone, joy lifting the pain in my head a little. "Actually, maybe we can all hang out one Saturday. If that's okay?"

"It is!" Bri says happily. "Thanks for telling me this, Nova. I don't want you to be sad. And soon it'll be summer and we can hang out every day and watch your girlfriend's softball games or whatever."

I smile at the idea. Me, Bri, maybe Tiffany and Skylar, cheering Lily on as she crushes softball (whatever that means; I've never seen a softball game before). We can get popcorn and candy, and after the game we can all hang out together.

Something that wouldn't be possible if I hadn't told Bri how I felt! I'm warm all over.

"Okay, deal. Now tell me about those cookies."

Bri chats to me about snickerdoodle cookies, her English test, and what Skylar said that made her laugh so hard, Sprite shot out of her nose and she had to change her uniform. And I listen, head pain easing, Kevin purring, and I don't get jealous even once.

CHAPTER 17

I stare down at my phone, a sick feeling in my stomach. That's been happening a lot lately.

I'm in Mr. Wickett's class, but I'm way early because Mrs. Warble lets us leave ten minutes early to "experience the world." I never know what she means by that, so I just go to class early and play on my phone. But today I'm on Kevin's Instagram, where there's a glaring comment under the latest picture.

Why did she post herself lol I came for the cat shes ugly

I look at the picture the comment references. It's the one Kylie took of me, where I'm holding Kevin in my lap. I don't think it's a bad picture. In fact, it's pretty good! My frown deepens at the word *ugly*. Doubt creeps into my mind. Maybe I should have cropped myself out and only showed Kevin.

I look up when Mr. Wickett says, "Good afternoon, Miss Weston." Lily says hi to him and then looks right at me. We both grin at the same time, and my stomach does a funny little flip as she approaches. It's been over a week since Lily became my girlfriend, but I still feel like I have a huge crush on her. Maybe I'll always feel this way! I smile even bigger at the thought.

Lily sits next to me, and we just stare at each other for a few seconds, smiling. Finally, she says, "Hey. How are you?"

"Good," I say. But then I remember my phone in my lap, and my smile fades.

Lily notices right away. Her smile fades into a frown, and she puts a hesitant hand on my arm. "No lying, remember. What's wrong?"

I sigh and show her the comment on my Instagram. Lily gasps with outrage.

"What a jerk! I can't believe he said that."

"Yeah. I think it's a pretty good picture."

"It's a great picture, and my girlfriend is *not* ugly." I'm surprised by the fierce passion in her voice. "Let me see your phone."

I give it to her, and she taps on the username: blu_skypeters. A picture of a middle-aged man with a beer gut pops up. He's holding a fish. Ugh. Mean *and* kills fish for fun.

"You're way cuter than him," Lily says. I smile at her as warm tingles of happiness vibrate in my body. She thinks I'm cute! Cuter than Blu Sky Man, granted, but cute all the same! She starts to say something else, but Mr. Wickett calls everyone to attention. She gives me my phone back, and I put it in my desk so he won't catch me.

"He's just jealous," Lily whispers while Mr. Wickett turns to write on the board. "And a loser because he's, like, super old and commenting on your post. Shouldn't he be at work or something?"

I let out a giggle and Mr. Wickett turns around. Lily and I look away from each other, pretending to take notes. When Mr.

Wickett turns back to the board, I sneak a look at Lily. She's taking notes fiercely, like she can channel all her anger into her pencil and onto the page. I smile down at my mess of numbers and random doodles. Lily is almost as mad as she was at my house, with Raina. She's angry because a random man was mean to me on the internet.

I might be the luckiest girl in seventh grade.

Twenty minutes later, after a bunch of notes and confusing numbers, Mr. Wickett passes back our homework. No . . . our tests! I wait, anxious, as he approaches my desk. He places Lily's test face down, but that doesn't mean anything; he always does that for everyone. He places mine face down too, and for some reason, he stares at me for a long moment. When he moves on to Kenny, I snatch my test off my desk and scan the top for the score.

78 percent.

A *78*. Seventy-eight. A C.

My breath gets short and there's a tinny, high-pitched screech in my ears. A C. I've never made a C in my life! How . . . did this happen? I know I was tired on the day of the test, but I studied so hard. I mean, I have been spending a lot of time online, managing Kevin's fame . . . and I had a biting headache when I took it, but I can't believe this. I've been studying so hard, staying up until two in the morning sometimes! I feel like I'm going to throw up.

"Overall, a disappointing result from you all," Mr. Wickett says, but I feel a stab in my heart, like he's talking directly to me. "Remember, Cs and below have to be signed by your parents."

Oh no. *No.* Mom cannot know about this. She cannot find out I made a C. My vision squeezes tight, like I'm in a tunnel, and it's suddenly hard to breathe.

I'm jolted out of my panic by Lily's hand on my arm. She looks nervous. "Nova, are you okay? You look like you're about to faint."

I feel like I might faint. But I just nod robotically as the bell rings and signals us to go to the next class. I try to stand, but my legs are Jell-O. I sit down hard in my chair. I think I'm stunned.

"Miss Harris."

I blink and Mr. Wickett is standing right in front of my desk. He stares down at me with his Laser Eyes, and I just can't stand it, I can't stand disappointing him—

"Chin up," Mr. Wickett says. I blink at him, half in fear, half in confusion. What . . . ? He's not angry with me? After he offered tutoring and I said no? Mr. Wickett continues, "We can't be perfect every time. You tried hard, and you should be proud."

Somehow, my breath loosens in my chest. He's not mad. He said I should be proud. But how can I be proud of a seventy-eight? A C?! How can I be proud of anything less than excellence? Mom won't be proud of me. She'll be ashamed. I've let her down, again.

"Thanks, Mr. Wickett," I manage. I want to believe him. I want to be proud. But the big red 78 sits heavy in my mind, and all the soothing words in the world can't save me from Mom when she sees it.

I stare down at my spaghetti, a sick, horrible feeling in my stomach. Mom is picking at hers too, frowning fiercely at her phone.

Something happened at work today, and they're making her work overtime to fix her coworker's mistake. She's in a terrible mood. She wouldn't even look at Kevin when she got home. She just heated up two Lean Cuisines for us. But they're spaghetti—with meat sauce. I can't even pick out the meat when it's in the sauce. This, on top of the mean comment and the seventy-eight, is too much. I'm nearly in tears. The Harris girls are not having a good day.

"I can't believe this," Mom mutters darkly. "I have to study! I have a test and they make me fix Fran's stuff."

I just stare down at my food. Fran is always ruining Mom's day. I met her once, and she was a snotty-looking lady who wore expensive suits we could never afford. She was definitely the type to leave mean comments on Instagram.

"This is why you have to study hard, Nova."

I look up and Mom is staring right at me. She's mad, almost volcano-level. I know she's not mad at me, but I still flinch.

"If I had a degree like Fran, I wouldn't have to do this. I could coast like she does." Her voice is tense and bitter. "This is why education is so important. If you don't study and work hard, you'll end up like this."

I sink down in my chair, the red 78 flashing like neon before my eyes. I wish Mom wouldn't say that. She may not like her job, but I still think she's amazing. I still think she's a hero. But she doesn't see it that way. And she definitely won't see my failure that way either. Kevin, who long since escaped baby jail and was prowling under the table in case we dropped something, puts his paws on my leg. I scratch his head and he rubs against my fingers, purring reassuringly.

Mom takes a deep breath. She puts her head in her hands and takes several more deep breaths. When she looks up, she doesn't seem mad anymore. Just really, really tired. Sympathy tugs at my eyes, forming more tears. I don't know which one is worse.

"I'm sorry, Nova, this is adult stuff." She stands and takes her picked-over spaghetti to the kitchen sink. "You finish eating and go upstairs, okay? It'll be better tomorrow."

I jump out of my chair and hurry to put my spaghetti with hers. "I'll go now. I'm not hungry."

I'm surprised when Mom frowns and touches my forehead. Her palm is cool against my skin. "You're not sick, are you? You're not warm."

"No, I'm just tired." I hesitate, then hug Mom with both my arms. "I'm sorry Fran is such a jerk."

I feel Mom chuckle under my cheek. She hugs me back. "It's okay. I shouldn't have said all that. It's adult business."

Yeah . . . I think uneasily about my test. I need her to sign it. Those are the rules. But I can't ask her now. She's tired and angry, and I just want to stay here forever, where she thinks I'm a smart daughter who's good at math, and she loves me. There's no way I can disappoint her tonight.

Mom kisses the top of my head. "Go to bed early tonight. You don't want to get sick."

I nod, and Mom breaks our hug to shoo me to my room. I climb the stairs, Kevin on my heels, and sit down at my desk. The test is right in front of me, mocking me. I need her to sign it. I can't let her find out.

I close my eyes. I have a headache again, throbbing right between my eyes. I know what I have to do, but I don't feel good about it.

I open my eyes, grab a pen, and write on my test, in careful cursive, *Deidre Harris*.

CHAPTER 18

The next day, I sit next to Lily at lunch. I brought a lunch, but it's just a bunch of snacks. I don't feel like salad today. My stomach is rolling and queasy, and it has been ever since I signed Mom's name on my test.

Lily frowns as I sit down. It's just us for now, but I see Raina approaching with her cute box. I feel like I need to apologize to her since I don't hate Tiffany anymore. The boxes really are cute.

"You okay?" Lily's voice is soothing and soft. "How'd it go with your mom and the test?"

"Good." My voice breaks though, and tears fill my eyes. Lily pats my back sympathetically.

"That bad, huh?"

I close my eyes. I want to tell her about what I did, but I'm so ashamed. I just can't answer.

"Whoa, what's going on?"

I open my eyes to Kylie's concerned face. Raina sits down next to her a few seconds later, both eyebrows raised in interest.

"Nova had a hard day yesterday," Lily says for me. She squeezes my hand under the table, and I hold on to her quiet reassurance. At least I have Lily.

"Was it about the last Wickett test?" Kylie asks. "I got a sixty-seven. Can you believe it? I even studied a little this time!"

It does make me feel a little better that Kylie also didn't do well. "What did your mom say?" I ask.

Kylie rolls her eyes. "You have to try harder, I'm gonna take your phone if you don't improve, blah blah." Kylie waves her phone in the air. "I still have it, so I'm considering it a win!"

Kylie doesn't look upset at all. I don't get how we can be so different. I shake my head. Maybe we're not though. Maybe Mom would say those things too, if I gave her the chance. But I think back to when I didn't get into private school, and I can't take that chance. I mean, I didn't take the chance. I turned in the test this morning. It's too late to take it back.

"Anyway," Kylie says when I'm quiet, "don't let it get you down. You're still cool to us!"

"Extremely," Lily says, smiling.

"Always," Raina says. She opens her box and I frown—it's full of just vegetables, no meat, no starch, no cookies. I feel like garbage, and I even brought Oreos.

Kylie notices at the same time I do. "What's with this depressing lunch? I swear, you and Nova kill me."

"You know Mom is on my case. She doesn't want me to get—"

Raina cuts herself off, but it's too late. I know what she was about to say, and based on the way Lily flinches, she does too. Earlier, I would have been anxious about this change in the friend group, but I'm so tired. Lily is amazing and fantastic, and I'm sick of people hurting her feelings.

"Raina, that's not cool."

Everyone looks at me, and I'm a little afraid, but I keep going. "You're my friend, but you're hurting Lily's feelings and that has to stop."

Raina looks miserable. "I know, I'm so sorry. My mom is just—"

"Maybe you should talk it out with your mom," Lily interrupts her. She grabs my hand under the table and it's sweaty and trembling against mine, but above the table, Lily is deadly calm. I can practically hear rumbles of ominous thunder. "But don't take it out on me. I'm fat, and I don't care, but I hate that you look at me like there's something wrong with me."

"I don't!" Raina protests. This is the loudest I've ever heard her voice. She actually looks a little panicked for once. "I just—I just want to be healthy. And that's not, um . . ."

Lily rolls her eyes. "You think starving yourself is healthy?

You think having juice for dinner every single night is healthy? You think being too tired to play tennis after school is healthy? Give me a break."

The silence is so thick at our table, it's unbearable. Lily is so tense, her nails are digging into the skin on the back of my hand. But I don't dare let go because this is huge.

Raina takes a shaky breath. "You're right." Her voice is pained and soft. "You're right, Lily. I'm sorry. I—I'll talk to Mom. And I won't ever bring it up again."

Lily's death grip cautiously relaxes around my hand. "And I'll come help you if you want. Or sneak you actual lunches. Whatever! You know I'll do anything for you, but I won't be disrespected by someone I call my friend, you know?"

Raina nods, tears in her eyes, and I look at Lily in awe. I was right. I really am the luckiest girl in seventh grade. I look to Kylie, whose eyes are huge, and Raina who looks sad but hopeful at the same time. I decide if Lily can be brave like this, even when she was scared, I can too.

"Umm," I pipe up in the silence, "since we're being honest, I'm a vegetarian."

There's a heartbeat of silence, and then Raina and Kylie burst into laughter.

"What?!" Kylie howls, doubled over. I smile nervously; I don't get what's so funny about that, but okay . . . "Oh no, I've been stuffing you full of meatballs for weeks! Why didn't you tell us earlier?"

"I thought you'd think I was weird," I admit.

"No weirder than everyone else," Kylie says, grinning. She slings her arm around Raina's shoulder. "I'm just glad everyone made up. This lunch table has been stressing me the heck out."

"Me too," Lily says. She smiles at all of us, even Raina.

"Wait, one more thing." Kylie looks at me, which kind of alarms me. "I'm sorry about the Instagram thing, Nova. That first day, I really did just want to get my picture on there."

Ah, I knew it. Hurt sneaks into my chest, but Kylie hurries to continue.

"I know it's not right, but I just wanted to promote my dad's bakery. It's not doing great, and I thought if I could get the word out . . . but that doesn't matter. You're my friend and I don't want you to think anything else."

I turn the apology over in my head, but I think it's okay. She apologized, and I forgive her. I nod, giving her a tentative smile. "Okay. Thanks for telling me that."

"No problem!" Kylie sighs heavily and opens her lunch box. "And now we can eat in peace! I swear, y'all are gonna kill me."

I smile at Lily. We let go of our hands and eat lunch together. And for a while, everything seems like it'll be okay.

After school, I'm waiting for the bus when Lily runs to my side. I blink at her, surprised; her dad usually picks her up. "What's up?"

"I'm riding home with you today," she announces. I smile, shaking my head. If I had a fraction of her confidence . . .

"Okay, but why?"

"You were my hero at lunch today." Lily grins at me and slips her hand into mine. "And you seem really stressed about the test. So I thought it would be fun if we just chilled today. Umm, if that's okay."

I squeeze her hand in mine. "That's okay with me."

We climb onto the bus together and chat on the way home. When we get there, I open the door to Kevin, who's yowling at me. Hungry already! He usually freezes when he sees Lily, but today he circles around her, purring and yelling at the top of his lungs for food.

"I think he finally likes me!" Lily pets his back, and he purrs harder.

"That's two of us!" I almost groan at my own terrible joke, but Lily laughs.

"Good to know. Kevin and Nova, my biggest fans."

We feed Kevin and end up on the couch. I scroll through Netflix, but there's not really anything I want to watch. I turn to ask Lily what she thinks, and Lily's staring at me intently.

"What?" I say, laughing nervously.

"What was wrong today?" Lily asks. "You seemed really sad."

I feel myself wilting. I didn't really want to talk about it before. But . . . I kind of do now. I keep seeing that red 78 and feeling that horrible nausea in my gut after signing Mom's name. It's horrible. I already told Bri and she said as *soon* as she gets back from the movies with her parents, we're having a long talk. But that won't be until tonight, past dinner. I kind of want to talk now.

"I made a seventy-eight on the math test." Telling the truth makes me feel a tiny bit lighter. Lily nods sympathetically.

"I saw. I mean, I wasn't being nosy. But I do sit right next to you."

I smile. "It's okay. That's not the point. I mean it is, because I can't make Cs."

"Why not?"

I start to answer but then hesitate. I can't really figure out a way to tell Lily about Mom, her volcano days and softer days, how she's my hero but also she scares me a little. "I just can't. So I had to forge Mom's signature."

"Oh, Nova." Lily looks so sad I almost want to cry. She opens her arms. "Come here."

I lean into her for a hug, and she holds me really tight. I swear she squeezes a few tears from my eyes. "I feel so bad about it. Like I've been sick all day."

"You might be regular sick," Lily says, her voice muffled by my hair. "You're kind of warm."

Aww man, just what I need—a cold on top of everything else. I hug Lily back, overwhelmed. Instagram, school, Mr. Wickett's class, and now this—it's too much.

"I'm so tired," I whisper, so soft I don't know if Lily can hear.

But she does hear me, because she lets go of our hug and stares into my eyes. "Let's rest, then."

"What do you mean?"

"I mean, let's chill. We don't have to do anything except watch TV. And I'll be quiet so you can take a nap."

I search her face for any trace of uncertainty, but Lily's eyes are clear and sure. "You'd do that?"

"Of course! Come on, let's get cozy." Lily and I go to my room for a few spare blankets, and then before I know it, I'm bundled up like a cozy burrito, Kevin purring on my lap, Lily's arm around my shoulder and her cheek pressed against my head.

"What's your least favorite Disney movie?" she asks, scrolling through Disney+.

"*Cars* . . . ?"

"Ka-chow! And good night." Lily and I giggle, and the opening of *Cars* starts to play. I feel my eyelids get heavy immediately.

"You'll wake me up before Mom gets home?" My words are just a sleepy mumble.

"Of course." Lily hugs me again, and I fall into a strange half sleep on her shoulder. Everything is quiet and muted, and I feel relaxed for the first time in forever.

Kevin is purring, but at some point, he stops and hops off the couch. I miss his weight, but I keep snoozing. I'm in and out of sleep, focusing on the feeling of Lily's hand on my head, her thumb tracing circles on my hairline. It kind of tickles, but I'm too sleepy to laugh. She stops, abruptly, and I wrinkle my nose. I didn't want her to stop.

"Umm, hi, Ms. Harris."

Why would Lily call me that? That's so weird. And why does she sound so nervous?

"Nova and I were just watching a movie."

Lily sounds . . . afraid. That wakes me up a little. Why is she scared? And why is she talking about me in third person?

Wait a minute. I'm not Ms. Harris.

My eyes fly open and I'm now wide-awake, blinking frantically into the sudden light. I sit up and look around—blankets, TV, Kevin purring and rubbing against a familiar pair of legs. My stomach drops to my toes as I lift my head and stare right into Mom's furious glare.

CHAPTER 19

I think I'm gonna pass out.

There are spots in my vision and my breath is pinched and short. I am *dead*. How did this happen?! Did we both fall asleep? Did Lily's dad forget to pick her up?

Mom stands between me and the front door, hands on her hips. She's not very tall, but right now she feels like a giant, and I am an ant. "Nova, you better explain what's going on right now."

I spring to my feet, dumping all the blankets on the floor. I'm in full panic mode; I don't have time to think. "This is Lily! We're working on a group project together." The lies come easy and fast as my brain scrambles to get me out of the deep, deep hole I'm in. "We have science together and our teacher paired us up."

Lily glances at me, but I barely register that her expression is kind of hurt. I'm too busy watching Mom glare down at me with her Laser Eyes.

"Doesn't seem like you were working to me."

"We were taking a break!"

Mom starts to say something else, but Lily's dad honks his horn. No! We were so close. We almost made it. Lily looks at me nervously. I owe it to her to deal with Mom.

"That's her dad," I tell Mom. "She was just leaving, see?"

"Right." Mom turns her Laser Eyes to Lily. "Lily, is it?"

"Y-yes ma'am." Lily's voice is higher pitched than normal. Some of the blind terror is fading, and I ache to hold her hand.

"You seem like a very nice and polite girl." Oh, that's good! Mom already likes her—"But Nova failed to tell you that she's not allowed to have guests when I'm not home."

"Sorry," Lily says, but Mom waves her off.

"It's fine. You girls stay here, and I'll have a word with your father." We don't say anything as Mom marches to the front door and leaves the house. I take a shaky breath and hold on to the edge of the couch.

"I am so dead," I whisper.

"Your mom is *intense*." Lily's voice is also a whisper.

"What happened?" I know I'm whining, but I can't help it. "Did you let me sleep for too long?"

Lily looks offended. "No way! Look at the time."

I fumble for my phone: 4:23. "Why is she home so early?!"

"I don't know!" Lily crosses her arms. She seems irritated now. "We should have known this would happen eventually though. Why were we sneaking around anyway?"

I stare at Lily, stunned. "Umm, do you see what just happened?"

"Yeah, but she's mad that you lied to her. Not that I'm here."

"No, trust me, she's mad that you're here." Though she did seem to like Lily, maybe. If I squint.

Lily seems upset. And I get it because I'm upset too, but I'm still freaking out. "Nova, did you even try to ask your mom if I could come over?"

I hesitate. I didn't. But she doesn't know how Mom is, or how important it is for me to be perfect. "No . . . but—"

"That's what I thought. I just—I'm frustrated. I really wanted to meet your mom, and she thinks I'm just some random girl from your class. You didn't even say I was your friend."

I don't know what to say. I was just trying to get out of trouble. I didn't mean to hurt Lily's feelings.

Mom comes back. She holds open the front door. "Come on, Lily. Your dad's ready to go."

"Yes, ma'am." Lily looks at me, her expression is hurt and sad. "See you later, Nova."

I want to call her back and say I'm sorry, but then Mom would wonder why. And I can't risk that. So I say nothing and just watch as Lily says a nervous goodbye to Mom and leaves my house. Kevin hops onto the windowsill and watches her go, meowing sadly and pawing at the glass.

Mom shuts the door and stares at me. I look at the floor. "Nova, I don't even know what to say."

The disappointment threatens to crush me into a tiny, pathetic ball. Tears prick my eyes.

"You know better! I understand you wanting to get ahead on your project, but you should have just stayed at school and I would have picked you up."

"Sorry," I mumble. I can't look at her. I know I'll cry.

Mom is quiet for a second, so I risk looking at her. She looks vaguely confused, like she isn't sure what to say. With a jolt, I realize this is the first time I've done something this bad. Well, the first time she's caught me.

"Okay," Mom says. She stands up taller and folds her arms. The Laser Eyes are back, and they're shining right on me. "No TV, phone, or computer—unless for school—for two weeks."

Okay, that's not so bad. I can live with that. I won't be able to text Bri or Lily, but I'll actually get a break from Kevin's Instagram. I nod, ashamed but also a little relieved.

"And no seeing Bri this Saturday."

"What?!" The word is out of my mouth before I can stop it. This isn't fair! I only get to see Bri once every two weeks! I have to go a whole month without seeing my best friend? And I can't even talk to her because Mom will have my phone.

"Actions have consequences, Nova."

But why?! Why is it such a big deal to have a friend over sometimes? Why did she have to come home early *today*? I need to talk to Bri. Lily is mad at me, and I'm so tired, and I just want my best friend.

"Mom, please, can I—"

"No." Mom isn't in the mood for negotiating. She points upstairs. "No more arguing. I'm so disappointed. Clean up the living room and then go upstairs until I call you."

There's nothing else I can do. I gather up the blankets and my things, and then I troop upstairs, head down. Kevin follows me, but even he can't cheer me up. I feel almost numb. Everything that could go wrong did. I lost my girlfriend, I let Mom down, and I messed up my Saturdays with Bri. I can't do anything right. I lie on my bed, face down, and want to sleep for a thousand years. Kevin curls up beside me, purring and rubbing his head against mine.

"Thanks, Kev." I sniffle but I can't cry yet. I still have my phone but not for long. I send a quick text to Bri.

Mom caught me and Lily

NO!!! Bri adds a bunch of crying emojis. *How bad?*

Grounded for two weeks. No phone. I can't see you Saturday either.

My screen blurs as tears fill my eyes. It's unfair. But then I remember what Lily said and that makes me cry even harder— maybe it is fair. If I hadn't lied, maybe Mom would have let Lily come over. Or even if she said no, maybe she would have let me go to Lily's. I didn't even ask, and now I've let everyone down. Mom for lying, Lily for making her feel like she doesn't matter to me, and Bri for getting her caught up in my punishment. I feel like the worst person in the world.

I'll call your mom every day to bother her. I smile at my phone. Bri is still on my side, even if I let her down. I cradle my phone, holding on to that. At least, I try. My head is pounding with sadness and probably my cold, so I put it to the back of my mind.

Falling asleep I text Bri. *See you in ten thousand years I guess I'll be waiting!*

I smile one more time, then fall into an uneasy sleep.

CHAPTER 20

I don't feel good at all.

I tossed and turned all last night. I didn't even come downstairs when Mom called me for dinner. And now my head is pounding when I wake up for school, and my face is hot and stuffy, like someone shoved cotton up my nose while I slept. Lily was right. I'm definitely sick.

"Nova!" Mom yells from downstairs. "Hurry, you'll miss the bus!"

I don't want to go to school. I don't want to even go

downstairs. My chest hurts, and I let out a tiny cough. Ugh. I just want to sleep.

But I can't. I have to go to school so I don't fall behind and mess things up. *Again*. I have to be brave and follow through. I sniff the snot back into my nose (gross), sit up in bed, and get ready for school. I wash my face, brush my teeth, and put on a heavy hoodie so I won't get cold. I stare at my door, a little dizzy, but determined. I can do this.

I can't do this.

All day, I've tried to say hi to Lily, but she just looks away. And in math, she doesn't even say a word to me. I'm so sad I could die. I really hurt her feelings, and I feel terrible, but I don't know what to say or do to fix it.

After class, Mr. Wickett calls my name. Lily finally looks at me, worry crossing her face, but she doesn't say anything. Still, I'm a little hopeful. Maybe it's not too late.

"Yes, sir?" I sniffle, on the edge of tears, and also because my nose is running a lot. I should have stayed home.

Mr. Wickett watches me carefully. He has his Laser Eyes out again. "I wanted to ask how you were feeling about the next section of the material."

Bad. So, so bad. I tried to take notes today, but my head was pounding, and I kept looking at Lily, hoping she would look at me too. I swallow hard, my throat sending needles of pain to my brain. "Umm . . . fine."

"Really." Mr. Wickett's Laser Eyes focus right on me. "Why don't you want a tutor, Miss Harris? You said embarrassment wasn't an issue."

I rock back on my heels. I don't want to say. But I'm so tired, and Mr. Wickett will definitely catch me at this point. Then I remember what Lily said, about not giving anyone a chance when I lie. I feel myself giving in, just a little. "I don't want my mom to know."

Mr. Wickett raises his eyebrows. "She'll be angry with you?"

"Yeah. No." I breathe out a breath. I know she has bad days, especially with her stressful job, but she might not be angry. I think about her reaction to seeing Lily, how she was almost con-fused about what to do. "I lied to her. I said I was doing well."

"Ah." Mr. Wickett nods. And . . . he puts the Laser Eyes away! Now he just looks normal, almost kind. "Well then, how about you leave it to me? I'll talk to your mom for you, tell her it's my idea, and frame it in a way that won't get you in trouble."

I blink at him in shock. He would do that? "Really?"

"Really. What do you say?"

I hug myself, my chest a little lighter. I can't believe it. I can't believe it! I told Mr. Wickett the truth and he wasn't mad. He's working with me so I can keep getting better at math. I nod, a lot happier than before. "Okay. I'll do it."

Mr. Wickett smiles. "I'm proud of you, Miss Harris. I know the material is hard, but I believe in you. And also . . ." Mr. Wickett reaches in his bag and withdraws a familiar test. He points at the signature I forged. "You are not very good at sign-ing your mother's name."

Panic and heat fill my face. He found out! "Am I in trouble?"

"You will be if you do it again." Mr. Wickett gives me a serious look but quickly smiles again, and it's so nice and kind I could cry. "I know not everyone has a perfect home life, and I knew you had to have a reason to do this. But if your mother is a safe person for you, I encourage you to be honest with her. You might be surprised by what she thinks."

I nod, even though I'm still terrified of the concept. Mr. Wickett writes me a pass for the next class (because I am definitely going to be late) and gives me a flyer about tutoring. The tutor's name is Nancy, and she's apparently really good at math. And it's free!

I hold the two pieces of paper in my hands, frozen in the hallway outside Mr. Wickett's class. I told the truth. I didn't lie. And I got something amazing out of it. I thought I would let Mr. Wickett down, but he didn't even care. He just helped me, even though he didn't have to.

"Nova?"

I look up in surprise, and Lily stands just a few feet away from me. She looks worried, really worried. "Are you okay?"

"I'm fine." But my voice breaks and I sniffle. I'm not fine. I think Mr. Wickett broke me. Because everything I thought I was doing might have been wrong.

Lily steps closer. She puts a gentle hand on my arm and looks me right in my eyes. "Nova, are you okay?"

I blink. She asked me twice. Just like Bri told her to do because I always lie the first time. My eyes fill with tears. "No," I whisper, and suddenly I'm crying, harder than I have in a long time.

Lily hugs me and I hug her back, and I just cry into her shoulder for a long time. She pats my back and makes soft *shh* noises, which make me cry even harder because she's supposed to be mad at me! I'm the worst girlfriend, the worst friend, the worst student, and the worst daughter, all at once.

When I can breathe okay again, I pull back. Lily brushes her thumbs under my eyes, wiping away my tears. Anxiousness is all over her face.

"What happened? Did Mr. Wickett find out about the signature? Are you expelled?!"

That gets an awful, barky laugh out of me. "I don't think you can get expelled from public school."

"You can!" Lily wipes my tears one more time. "Talk to me, Nova. And don't lie this time, please. What happened?"

"I was wrong." I sniff, wishing I had a tissue. "I was wrong about everything. I should have told Mr. Wickett that I needed a tutor weeks ago, and then I wouldn't have gotten a seventy-eight. And I should have told Bri I was jealous of Tiffany sooner, because she didn't even care and offered to hang out more." I hiccup, fresh tears blooming. "And I shouldn't have tried to hide that I was dating you from Mom. Because I like you a lot, and I'm so sorry I hurt you, and I'm just a rotten person to everyone."

"You're not a rotten person." Lily fidgets, her gaze lowered to the ground. "I feel kind of rotten for avoiding you today. I wanted to make up, but I was still mad at you."

"Are you mad now?"

"No." Lily smiles, looking up again. "I got so nervous about Mr. Wickett finding out about the signature that it scared all the mad out of me."

I laugh and she does too, but mine ends in a horrible, wheezy bark. Lily hugs me again, and then presses her hand to my forehead.

"Hate to say it, but I think you've got a fever."

"You were right again," I mumble. I'm so relieved that Lily isn't mad at me anymore that I feel close to fainting. Actually . . . my vision gets dark spots all over, and they're dancing around so fast, I'm dizzy.

"Nova?" Lily's voice is far away.

"I think I need to sit down." I think I say that, but I'm not sure because the next thing I know, all the black dots merge and become one endless patch of darkness.

"Nova? Can you hear me?"

I open my eyes, bright light blinding me. I blink, rapidly, until I'm looking into the face of Mrs. Helen. Where am I? What happened?

Mrs. Helen smiles down at me. "Good girl! Thought I was gonna have to call an ambulance."

"Is she okay?" a worried voice next to my ear says. It takes me a second, but then I recognize it as Lily's, and that clears some of the grogginess. I must be in the nurse's office. I'm lying down on my back on a cot, covered with a thin blanket. I'm still freezing though.

"She's fine," Mrs. Helen says. "Probably has the flu. It's been going around. Nova, you conscious?"

"Yeah." My voice is rough and scratchy. I feel sick, but then everything comes back and I honestly feel more relieved. Lily and I made up. I'm getting a math tutor. Everything is almost okay. I sit up, but I immediately feel dizzy.

"Careful!" Mrs. Helen scolds me. "I called your mother. She'll be here to pick you up soon." She taps the top of my head with her pen. "You better not come here with a fever that high again, young lady."

"Sorry," I mumble.

Mrs. Helen loses interest and soon goes outside to talk to someone. I look at Lily and she sighs heavily. "You scared me to death, you know that?"

"Sorry," I say again. I'm apologizing an awful lot lately.

"It's okay." Lily climbs onto the side of the cot and gives me a one-armed hug. "I'm sorry you're sick, but now you can rest. You said you were tired, right?"

"I am. I really am."

I hear hurried footsteps outside and Mom's frantic voice. Lily takes her arm away and hops off my cot, pretending she's just standing next to me. Pretending she doesn't mean anything to me, even though she, Mom, and Bri are the most important people in my life.

Mom opens the door. She looks panicked, like there's a fire or something. She runs to me and holds my face in her hands. "Nova? Are you all right? They called me and told me you fainted!"

"I did," I say. "I think."

Mom isn't listening. She's checking my temperature with the back of her hand and groaning in dismay. She hugs me to her side and starts talking to Mrs. Helen, who's trying to calm her down.

I meet Lily's eyes. She smiles at me and mouths, "You okay?"

I smile back and nod, and for once, I'm not lying.

"Come on," Mom says to me. She hugs me and kisses the top of my head, and for a second it's like the old days, before I had to worry so much. "I'll call the doctor in the car."

"Okay." I get off the cot and Mom seems to finally notice Lily.

"Oh, Lily! Thank you for taking care of Nova."

"No problem, Ms. Harris." Lily waves a little to me. "See you later? Probably not tomorrow. But soon?"

I could just wave so Mom won't be suspicious, but suddenly, I really don't care. I want to hug Lily, so I do, as tight as I can. "I'll see you later."

When I turn back to Mom, she has a weird expression on her face, but it's quickly replaced by worry again. She hurries me out of the office, and as Lily disappears behind me, I know what I have to do.

I have to tell Mom everything.

CHAPTER 21

Mom glances at me in the rearview mirror. We're on the way back from the doctor. I had to wait a miserable hour, but I finally saw Dr. Parker, and he diagnosed me with the flu and sent me home with some cough medicine. Mom wasn't really happy, but what can you do? At least I don't have to go back to school and I can rest, like Lily said.

I'm also thinking about another thing Lily said, about me. And how I should be brave. It may be the fever, but I do feel brave. I was scared of Mom and that she'd be disappointed in me, and maybe she will be. But this is the last step. I was able to be honest with everyone else, so I just have to face Mom. It's scary, but Bri, Lily, Kylie, Raina, and even Mr. Wickett care about me. The real me. I think Mom will too. At least, I hope she will.

"Mom, I have to tell you something."

"Okay," Mom says. She sounds guarded, but she doesn't seem mad. "What's up? Besides getting you home, eating some soup, and going to bed."

That gives me a little courage. Mom cares about me too. I hesitate, trying to pick the easiest thing to start with. "I'm . . . kind of struggling in math."

Mom glances at me in the mirror again. I wait for an explosion, or for her to yell that I'm not trying, but it doesn't happen. She just says, "Okay. When you're feeling better, we can look at it together. Or do you want me to find you a tutor?"

"I did already," I say quickly. "Well, Mr. Wickett did. It's free!"

"Great." Mom nods, and she even smiles. "We'll get that started soon. But only after you've kicked the flu."

I wait for more, but Mom returns her attention to the road and doesn't say anything. After a tense minute, I ask, "Are you mad?"

Mom glances back at me again. She's frowning this time. "No. Why would I be mad? You have a problem, but you're already taking steps to fix it. That's a good thing!"

Oh. I smile a little, and Mom smiles back. This is going really well so far! But everything else is so hard. And I don't know what steps to take to fix the rest.

"I have something else to tell you."

"Okay." Mom is smiling now, like she's amused. I hope she keeps smiling.

"I'm a vegetarian." It comes out in a rush, and my heart is beating really fast. "I don't eat meat and I don't want to. And my favorite pizza isn't pepperoni. It was, but not anymore."

Mom raises her eyebrows and is silent for a few seconds. Then she says, "Okay . . . what made you decide that?"

I tell her about greenhouse gases and animal cruelty and everything I've already told Bri and Lily. She listens, and I don't realize how long I've been talking until she pulls into our driveway.

Mom parks, then turns to face me. She doesn't look mad at all! Just kind of curious. "How long have you been a vegetarian?"

"A year, I guess."

"What have you been doing with all the meat at dinner?"

I stare down at my lap. "I just . . . don't eat it. Or I give it to Kevin."

"No wonder that cat is so huge," Mom mutters. "Nova, look at me."

I do, reluctantly, and Mom's face is serious. "Why didn't you tell me you didn't want to eat meat? We've wasted a lot of food in a year."

Oh no, this is it. I knew it was going too well. I'm so nervous, my eyes fill with fearful tears. But I want to be honest with her, even if it's scary. "I'm sorry. I didn't want you to be mad at me. Or . . . or disappointed."

Mom narrows her eyes. Her Laser Eyes. And I'm caught right in their beam. "Why are you telling me this right now?"

I swallow the little spit remaining in my mouth, and my sore throat protests. "Because . . . I have a lot to tell you."

Mom turns off the car. "Let's go inside, and then we'll talk." Her voice is neutral, but I can't help shaking in fear and anticipation. She waits for me to get out of the car before locking it, and then we go inside the house together. She steers me to the couch, gets me some water and medicine, and then sits in the armchair across from me. Her expression is intense, but I try my best to be brave.

"All right, Nova." Mom nods. "Start from the beginning."

And I do. I tell her everything. I tell her about the secret Instagram, Kevin's fame, and the horrible, unmanageable comments that came with it. I tell her that I let Kylie and Raina come over, and that I think we're friends, but it didn't start that way. I tell her that I like girls, maybe, but I really like Lily, and she likes me too. That's the hardest one. Mom just listens, stone-faced, but when I get to Lily, surprise crosses her face before it settles back into stone. Is that good or bad surprise? I can't tell and I'm so scared, but I keep going until it's all out.

When I finish, Mom doesn't say anything for an entire minute. I'm sweating a lot now, so much I'm sure my shirt is soaked under my hoodie. My body trembles with fear and nausea. That might be from the flu though.

Finally, Mom speaks. "I think you should go to your room."

I burst into tears. I can't help it. She hates me. I was brave, but I should have just kept this to myself because—

"Come here, Nova." Mom's voice is soft, and suddenly she's hugging me. I cling to her shirt, sobbing, my heart in tiny, shattered pieces.

"I'm s-so sorry," I sob. "Please don't hate m-me."

"I don't hate you. Hush that crying, come on." Mom wipes my face, and I try to stop crying, but it's hard. Mom lifts my chin so I'm looking at her face. "Are you listening to me?"

I nod, unable to speak.

"I don't hate you. I love you, and there's nothing that could change that. You understand?"

I nod again, hope springing into my chest.

"But I am angry that you lied to me. Repeatedly. For a long time now." Mom takes a deep breath. "I don't want to make any hasty decisions while I'm upset. And you're upset too, so we need to cool off now and come back later."

I nod, but I don't want to cool off. I want to sit in Mom's lap like I'm little again and have her hold me tight and never let go. Mom kisses my forehead, then presses the back of her hand to the spot she just kissed. She makes a dissatisfied sound in her throat.

"Let's get some medicine in you and then take a nap, all right?"

"Okay." My voice is small and scratchy. "I'm sorry, Mom. I love you."

"I love you too."

Mom gives me cough syrup and makes me drink half a

bottle of water. She leads me to my room and makes me change clothes, and soon I'm wrapped in my softest pajamas and snuggled under the covers, Kevin curled by my side.

Mom smooths my hair away from my face. She doesn't seem mad, but I'm so tired and afraid, I can't really tell.

"Sleep," Mom says. "When you wake up, we'll talk. Okay?"

"Okay." I keep my eyes open to watch Mom leave, but she doesn't. She stays next to me while my eyelids get heavier and heavier, and soon I'm asleep.

CHAPTER 22

I wake up to a rumbling sound.

I blink groggily, trying to understand what's happening, and the rumbling gets louder. I feel the vibrations on my chest, and when I open my eyes all the way, all I see is Kevin's giant butt in my face.

I laugh, then wince as pain stabs through my lungs. Ugh, I feel horrible.

Then I remember what happened, and I feel worse.

I lie still for at least twenty minutes, too tired and scared to move. Kevin just keeps purring away on my chest, occasionally kneading his claws into my comforter. "Thanks, buddy." My voice is a whisper.

I start to doze back off but stiffen when the door creaks open and light from the hallway spills into my darkened room. Mom peeks in, and I'm half scared and half relieved she's here.

"Nova?" she whispers.

I could pretend to be asleep, but if we don't talk soon, I think I'll die of anticipation. I wave a little, and Mom comes into the room. She touches my forehead and nods, looking relieved.

"Your fever is down."

"That's good." I cough weakly, disturbing Kevin. He lets out a disapproving huff and settles back on my chest.

"You're gonna suffocate with this guy on you." Mom chuckles, then carefully lifts Kevin from my chest. He dangles in her arms, ears pulled back in annoyance, but he doesn't bite or scratch her. She puts him on the ground, and he flounces to my closet, where he collapses on a pile of my stolen clothes.

"You picked him up." I can't keep the awe out of my voice. Mom's never picked up Kevin! She's always been too afraid.

Mom smiles. "There's a lot I'd do for you." Mom hesitates, then smooths my hair back. "You ready?"

I close my eyes. This is it. "Okay."

"All right. Let's go downstairs." Mom waits for me as I get up and get out of bed. I go to the bathroom and brush my teeth, and it almost feels like I'm getting ready for school . . . and not a big, scary talk that will affect my entire life. I look in the mirror at my flushed face and wide eyes. I take a deep breath. I can do this. I have to.

Mom leads the way downstairs and gets me some water and more cough syrup. I sit on the couch again, her in the armchair, and I wait for her to start.

Mom sighs, like she's nervous. Maybe this is hard for her too. "Okay. I thought about what you told me, and we just need to have a conversation about it. Because I was angry, but now I'm confused."

I nod, not trusting my voice.

"Let's start with the easiest one. That Instagram has to go."

I hang my head in shame. I knew that would happen, but it

still stings. I wish everything hadn't gotten so out of control. "Okay, I understand."

"I don't think you do." Mom blows out a breath. I'm reminded of a volcano releasing steam, and I pull my blanket up to my chin. "You know social media is against the rules. Social media is against *their* rules too—you have to be thirteen to have an account, and you're not. Why did you disobey me?"

I shrug, kicking my feet. The impulse is to lie, but I don't want to do that anymore. Plus, I'm already in trouble anyway. I might as well be honest. "Bri has one, and I like to see the pictures of her new school and her new friends."

"First of all, Bri won't have one for long." I wince. Sorry, Bri. Looks like we will be double killed after all. "And second, you have Bri's number. You can just text each other or send each other pictures."

"I know. I guess . . . I guess I didn't see why it was a bad thing."

"Do you see now?" Mom holds out my own phone to me, where she highlighted the mean message from blu_skypeters. I don't take it; I just nod, misery hitting me all at once. Mom was right, and I didn't listen, and I paid for it.

Mom looks upset too. "I don't like strangers talking to you like this, Nova. Have you seen all these DMs?"

"No . . . there were too many so I didn't open them."

"Good, because there are some nasty things in here. Some of these people are sick, and they're trying to take advantage of you because you're young. *That's* why I said no social media." Mom releases a calming breath again, and for the first time I realize she might not be mad. I think she's upset by the mean comments. "I'm your mother. I'm trying to keep you safe. But I can't keep you safe when you do these things behind my back. I can't keep you safe when you don't listen to me."

"I'm sorry," I murmur, and I really am. I loved my Instagram, but lately it hasn't been fun anymore.

"I know. So when we get done talking, we'll save all the pictures and videos, and then we're deleting it together."

"Okay." I hesitate, but add, "I'm kind of glad. It was really hard to keep up with. Like having a job."

Mom cracks a smile at that. "I believe it. School is your job, okay? Leave the influencer thing for when you're an adult."

I nod. Kevin being famous was fun for, like, three days, but I'm relieved to see it go. Now he can be regular Kevin again.

"You've also lost your phone privileges until I can trust you again. You can have it for an hour a day, *after* homework is done, and I will be checking it every night. Do we understand?"

I nod. I'm bummed, but at least she'll let me talk to Bri and Lily for an hour. That's a good thing.

"All right, that's settled. Let's move on to Lily."

I freeze, fear in my heart. I don't know if I'm prepared for this.

Mom looks at me, then takes my hands in hers. She stares right into my eyes. "First, I love you. And while I am surprised to learn you're queer, I don't care who you like. That's not the issue here, and I just want to make that clear."

I nod, tears in my eyes. "Okay."

"I'm concerned that you felt like you couldn't tell me. Before yesterday, I'd never even seen Lily. I've never even heard you talk about having a crush on anyone. Why do you feel like you can't talk to me about this?"

"Technically, you did see her. She was at the park with me and Bri that time." Mom just raises one eyebrow at my weak joke. I look down, feeling awkward and happy and confused. "I . . . I don't know. It's weird to talk about this stuff with your mom."

Mom chuckles. "Fair enough."

"And," I say, a little emboldened by her laughter, "you always said I can't date until I'm sixteen. I thought you'd just say no."

Mom is quiet for a few seconds, so I look up. I'm surprised to see how sad she looks. "That's my fault. I should have told you why I have that rule."

Mom sighs and sits up in her chair. "When I was just a little older than you, I was boy crazy. Having a boyfriend was all I could think about. And that led me down a path I'm not proud of."

"What do you mean?"

"I mean I was distracted. Not focused on the things that

mattered, like school. And I was vulnerable. I thought I knew everything. I didn't. I started dating someone way older than me, and he took advantage of me. I let him distract and hurt me, and I should have left, but I didn't have the strength. And when I found out I was pregnant, suddenly he was missing in action." Mom sighs again. "I want better for you, Nova. That's why I push you so hard. You're smart and talented, and I don't want you to make the same mistakes I did. I didn't have a mom to tell me when I was slipping. Mine was either gone partying or had her head in the clouds. So when I had you, I promised myself I would be more attentive and set you on the right path." Mom struggles for words for a second, like what she's saying is painful. "But I messed up somewhere along the way, and I made you feel like you couldn't be honest with me. And for that, I'm so sorry."

I want to cry. I didn't know any of this. Mom never, ever wants to talk about my dad or my grandparents. I've never even met them. I guess I know why now. I stand up and hug Mom as tight as I can.

"I love you," I say. "And I'm sorry my dad sucks. And your

mom was such a jerk. You're way better than both of them put together."

Mom laughs and hugs me back. She kisses my temple, and I swear I hear her sniffle. I've never seen Mom cry. I might start if she does, so I just hold her close for a long time.

Eventually, Mom lets me go. She kisses my head again, and I've never felt so loved. "Now, let's set some boundaries. I can tell that Lily makes you happy, and even though I'm not happy about you dating so young, she seems like a nice girl. I want to meet her parents—properly this time, not just hanging out of a truck—and when she comes over, I have to be home and the door to your room has to be open. No exceptions."

"You won't make me break up with her?" My heart is so full of hope. I can't believe it! I thought for sure it would be over.

Mom smiles. "You don't have to break up with her. But you will if you don't respect our new boundaries."

"Okay!" I'm so happy I could spontaneously combust. Another good vocab word!

"Last one. These new friends who have been to my house

multiple times." Mom doesn't look impressed. Uh-oh. "I'm assuming they're the ones on your Instagram?"

"Yeah . . ."

"Are they nice to you? Or do they just like that you have a semi-famous cat?"

"No, they're nice! I think . . . I think they might be my real friends now."

"Okay. So why did you hide them from me?"

"I didn't mean to." I look for a way to explain, but it's hard. "I'm just . . . I'm really lonely at school without Bri. I mean, I was. I didn't have any other friends, and I just wanted them to like me so bad that when they asked to come over, I felt like I couldn't say no."

Mom looks troubled. "I didn't know you were having trouble making friends."

"Yeah . . . I didn't want to worry you. And I know it's my fault that me and Bri got separated, so—"

"Wait, stop," Mom interrupts. "What do you mean it's your fault?"

"Because I wasn't smart enough for the private school." I fidget in my seat, shame heating my cheeks. I guess I have one last thing I should confess. "I've been trying really hard to study for the retest. I planned on taking it and surprising you, but now I'm not sure I want to go to a different school . . . but anyway, that's why I was studying so much, and I didn't want to tell you about math. Or my new friends."

Mom's expression twists from confusion into pain. She looks like she's about to cry. "Oh, Nova, no. That's not why you didn't get to go."

"But I thought . . ."

Mom shakes her head. "I see now that I've got to be more transparent with you too. You're old enough to know the truth." Mom looks right into my eyes again, her face serious. "You *are* smart enough to go to private school. You and Bri got very similar scores on the entrance exam. But you didn't get to go because I can't afford it."

"Oh." That . . . makes a lot of sense. I should have known that private school is a lot of money. I'm so relieved—I am smart enough!

But Mom doesn't seem relieved. She looks really sad. "I'm sorry, Nova. I've tried very hard to make sure that you don't feel different than your classmates. But Bri has two parents, and loving grandparents who are thrilled to help pay tuition. But we can't do that. It's just me." Mom's eyes get wet with tears. "I'm sorry I let you down."

I want to cry too. This whole time I thought I was letting Mom down, and she thought the same thing. "You didn't let me down, Mom, I promise! I don't have to go to a private school or anything. I'm okay where I am." And, weirdly, that feels true. Two months ago, I would have given my left kidney to go to Bri's school. But now I have friends, and Lily, and I guess I don't need to follow Bri everywhere. We're still best friends, even if we don't go to the same school. Everything's okay. "In fact, I always think I let you down."

"Why would you think that?"

I squirm in my seat. "Because I'm bad at math. Before I got a tutor, I got a C on my test." I wince, waiting for an explosion.

Mom doesn't explode. She just . . . smiles? "Let me show you something."

Mom pulls out her phone and touches the screen a few times. Then she turns the screen around to face me. I hold it, confused. It's a list of . . . grades? For people I don't know. And Mom has highlighted her name, and next to it is . . . "a seventy-two?!"

I look up at Mom in shock, but she just shrugs, smiling. "I had a hard week. Things were going wrong at work and I didn't have time to study. So I got a C." Mom moves from the armchair to the couch and hugs me with one arm. "I did the best I could at the time. I have to be proud of that. And if you are doing your best, I will always be proud of you."

I hug Mom, overwhelmed with emotion. She's still my hero. But she's not perfect; she gets mad sometimes, and hides things from me, and makes Cs on her tests. And now I don't feel so scared of her. She's just Mom, and she loves me, and she said nothing can ever change that. I bury my face in her side and let out a few tears while she strokes my hair.

"Am I still in trouble?" I mumble.

"Oh yeah," Mom says, a laugh in her voice. "Big trouble. But for now, let's eat some dinner and go to bed."

I look up at her and she wipes my eyes with her thumbs, a gentle expression on her face. "While you were sleeping, I looked up some vegetarian recipes. I don't know how to use tofu yet—sounds pretty scary, if I'm honest—but I'm pretty confident in my fried rice skills. What do you say?"

I grin at her and, somehow, I feel like everything is going to be okay. "I'd really like that."

EPILOGUE

Two Months Later

Bri shakes a pack of peanut butter M&M'S in my face. I hold my hand out as she pours some into my palm, squinting against the bright sun. "I don't know about this softball thing."

"You mean this 'being outdoors' thing," Kylie teases. She bumps her knee against mine, but I'm startled so I drop all the M&M'S Bri gave me. They clatter down the bleachers to the ground, and Bri howls in anguish. "My allowance!" Kylie and I start laughing, and Raina and Skylar do too.

I'm at the softball fields, crowded on hot metal bleachers, sun beaming unforgivingly above . . . and I wouldn't rather be anywhere else. After Mom and I talked, my life got so much better. I kicked the flu and introduced Mom to my new friends and girlfriend. I stopped worrying so much about being perfect and just tried to do my best. I met with Nancy the tutor, about math, and aced Mr. Wickett's final exam. The best 89.7 I've ever earned. I think I'll frame my final report card and hang it above my desk to remind myself nothing can ever be as hard as that class. And I got through it anyway.

It wasn't all perfect. When I got a C on a pop quiz on *A Dog Called Kitty*, I had a meltdown and Lily had to sit with me in the bathroom for two class periods while I panicked. I met Tiffany and her boyfriend, but she made fun of my old shoes so I told her that her bento boxes were stupid. I'm not proud of that, and Bri was so mad we couldn't get along that she didn't talk to me for a week. She didn't talk to Tiffany either though, so at least it was fair.

But even though life hasn't been perfect, I don't think it has to be. In fact, I think it's better. I'm hot and M&M'S-less now, but I'm hanging out with my best friends, watching my girlfriend run around bases, and I'm happier than I've been in years.

"Have you decided what you're doing for your birthday, Nova?" Skylar asks me. Unlike Tiffany, Skylar is cool; he's super into baking, and he helped me with my final project for home ec. Sometimes, Bri invites Skylar to our Saturday hang outs, and I really look forward to seeing him.

"Probably studying," Raina says, sipping water from her trusty thermos.

"No way, this is the big one! You'll be officially thirteen!" Bri says. She leans over and offers Raina some M&M'S. Raina hesitates but accepts a few. She meets my eyes as she pops them into her mouth, and we smile at each other. She's doing better too.

"Actually . . ." I fidget against the bleachers. I asked Mom a hundred times if she was sure, so much she got annoyed. Lily and I practiced this last night, so I can't be nervous. I can do this. "I was wondering if you guys wanted to come to my house next weekend? Mom says you can't sleep over, but I'm pretty sure we'll have cake."

"Umm, obviously," Kylie says. "Ooh, my dad can bake your cake!"

"I'm coming too," Raina says, smiling.

"Me too," Skylar says. "I can't wait to meet the formerly famous Kevin."

"Yes!" Bri shouts. She hugs me, and I laugh. "I'm so proud of you!"

My face fills with happy heat as my friends—my real friends—accept my invitation. A few months ago, I was sad and lonely, unable to be honest with anyone, including Mom. But now I'm surrounded by people who like me, people who don't expect me to be perfect, and Mom trusts me enough to have an actual thirteenth birthday party. I still don't have my phone back but hey, baby steps.

My friends and I cheer on Lily and her team, the PowerPuff Girls, and when Lily hits a home run, I scream so loud I'm sure I pull a muscle in my neck. After the game is over, I run to the dugout, dodge Lily's disgruntled (vocab word!) coach, and leap into her arms. She laughs and hugs me back.

"You hit a home run!" I yell in her ear. Her whole team is celebrating, hugging and screaming and meeting their families on the field.

"I did!" Lily bounces with excitement and squeezes me tight.

"I'm so proud I'm gonna faint."

"Please don't." Lily laughs and kisses me, right in front of everyone. I'm so happy and dazzled I can barely believe it. My new shirt is dirty now from the dusty field, and I don't even care.

After we break apart, we just look at each other. I take in Lily's big brown eyes, the round cheeks I love, the smudge of dirt on her cheek. I can't stop smiling. "I asked everyone if they wanted to come to my party."

"And?" Lily's expression is hopefully curious, but she can barely contain the excitement in her voice.

"They said yes."

"Yes!" Lily shouts just like Bri did, and we're laughing again. For a second, I pause and look at my life and how much happier I am, and I'm so glad I don't have to lie anymore. I feel like the luckiest almost-thirteen-year-old in existence.

Lily's parents meet us on the field, and her dad is so happy about winning that he hugs me and Lily at the same time, spinning us around in a circle. Her mom scolds him, and Lily groans, embarrassed. All my friends arrive too, and we all hug, one big sweaty messy pile of love.

"Who wants Dairy Queen?" Lily's dad announces. We all cheer in agreement, Bri loops her arm with me, and Lily's hand slips into mine. I hold Lily's hand tight, bump my hip into Bri's, and I head to Dairy Queen with the best people in the world.

ACKNOWLEDGMENTS

For the third time, and probably forever, the biggest thanks goes to Grandma. You're a miraculous combination of grandmother, mother, and best friend, and I love you more than I could ever put into words. I love our recreational fights and I appreciate you listening to my wild story ideas, even the cat ones.

Thanks to my incredible agent, Holly Root! Fierce advocate, excellent business partner, overall greatest agent in the world. I hope we continue to have many more books together! Also huge thanks to my editor, Talia Seidenfeld! I so enjoyed working with you to bring Nova's story to life, and your editorial eye is unmatched. This is our first book together but hopefully not the last! Thanks are also in order to the entire Scholastic team.

To my best friend, Emily Chapman—your unwavering support is much appreciated. I love talking about cats and movies and everything else with you. I also love exchanging cat pictures! A.Z. Louise, thank you as well for always accepting my 3 a.m. screaming DMs about my next big book idea. If we could bottle the sheer amount of hype we generate while discussing snakes, Pokémon, and wild speculative story ideas, we would be very rich.

Thank you to my many writing groups: Scream Town, the slackers, WiM, Horror-Romance Alliance. I genuinely couldn't do this job without your cheers and support. And a list of people who have always been there for me, in no particular order: Tas, Mary Roach, Gigi Griffis, Zoe Zander, Chandra Fisher, Ashton Webb, Belinda Grant, Melissa, and Linnea Schiff.

Recently, I've realized how solitary writing really is. It can be lonely, but it's also shown me that it takes more than people to get you through the difficult days. So, thank you to the two stray cats I feed, Thomas and Butter, for bringing me joy and a reason to get out of bed each day. Thank you to sunsets and sunrises, cold noodles at midnight and sweet tea, family events, and new experiences. Thank you to *Kitchen Nightmares*, which I have seen all 102 episodes five times. Thank you to new music I play on repeat until I'm sick of it, to horror shows that make me stay up until daylight because I'm a wimp, to sitting in silence and, somehow, knowing everything will be okay.

And, finally, thank you to younger me. You stayed, and though times are hard, I know you're glad you were able to see how far we've come.

Find more reads you will love . . .

Avery Williams loves to sing, but that doesn't mean she wants to be on stage. When she gets roped into auditioning for the school's musical by Nic, her crush, she's definitely not expecting to land the lead role! She knows she should be excited, but Avery is mostly terrified. With the help of Nic and a stray cat, Avery must learn how to step out from backstage and into the spotlight.

Janie believes that with a strict schedule and organization, you can do anything. So when her new stepmom and her daughter, Makayla, move in with Janie and her mom, she's in for an unpleasant surprise. Worst of all? They're bringing a cat. Janie tries to be a good sister and welcomes Makayla with open arms. But when all of her friends start paying more attention to Makayla, Janie feels like she's being replaced. What's a gal to do with a copycat in her life?

Hedge
Over
Heels

Sometimes the
prickliest friends have
the biggest hearts.

Elise McMullen-Ciotti

SCHOLASTIC

Rayna is used to being the new kid at school, but that doesn't mean she wants to make new friends! Why bother when the military will only reassign her mom again soon anyway? The only friend Rayna wants is a furry, four-legged one. But instead of the dog she's been dreaming of, Rayna gets a hedgehog named Spike who is just as prickly and emo as she is. Worse, Rayna's mom insists she enter Spike in a pet talent show to get to know some kids her age, including a very cute boy named Nick. Will Rayna curl herself into a ball and hide, or will she and Spike take a chance a new pack of friends?

Have you read all the wish books?

☐ *Allie, First at Last* by Angela Cervantes

☐ *Gaby, Lost and Found* by Angela Cervantes

☐ *Lety Out Loud* by Angela Cervantes

☐ *Keep It Together, Keiko Carter* by Debbi Michiko Florence

☐ *Just Be Cool, Jenna Sakai* by Debbi Michiko Florence

☐ *This Is How I Roll* by Debbie Michiko Florence

☐ *Alpaca My Bags* by Jenny Goebel

☐ *Pigture Perfect* by Jenny Goebel

☐ *Sit, Stay, Love* by J. J. Howard

☐ *The Love Pug* by J. J. Howard

☐ *11 Birthdays* by Wendy Mass

☐ *Finally* by Wendy Mass

☐ *13 Gifts* by Wendy Mass

☐ *The Last Present* by Wendy Mass

☐ *Graceful* by Wendy Mass

☐ *Twice Upon a Time: Rapunzel, the One with All the Hair* by Wendy Mass

Read the latest books!

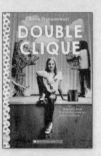